One-of-a-Kind MALLIE

OTHER YEARLING BOOKS YOU WILL ENJOY:

RUTHIE'S GIFT, *Kimberly Brubaker Bradley*
CHEAPER BY THE DOZEN, *Frank B. Gilbreth, Jr., and Ernestine Gilbreth Carey*
THE SMUGGLERS, *Iain Lawrence*
THIRD GRADE PET, *Judy Cox*
JOURNEY TO NOWHERE, *Mary Jane Auch*
LILY'S CROSSING, *Patricia Reilly Giff*
BESS'S LOG CABIN QUILT, *D. Anne Love*
DAKOTA SPRING, *D. Anne Love*
THREE AGAINST THE TIDE, *D. Anne Love*
NORTH BY NIGHT: A STORY OF THE UNDERGROUND RAILROAD, *Katherine Ayres*
FAMILY TREE, *Katherine Ayres*

YEARLING BOOKS are designed especially to entertain and enlighten young people. Patricia Reilly Giff, consultant to this series, received her bachelor's degree from Marymount College and a master's degree in history from St. John's University. She holds a Professional Diploma in Reading and a Doctorate of Humane Letters from Hofstra University. She was a teacher and reading consultant for many years, and is the author of numerous books for young readers.

One-of-a-Kind
MALLIE

Kimberly Brubaker Bradley

A Yearling Book

Published by
Dell Yearling
an imprint of
Random House Children's Books
a division of Random House, Inc.
1540 Broadway
New York, New York 10036

Visit us on the Web! www.randomhouse.com/kids

Educators and librarians, for a variety of teaching tools, visit us at www.randomhouse.com/teachers

---

ISBN 0-440-41623-X

Reprinted by arrangement with Delacorte Press

Printed in the United States of America

October 2000

10 9 8 7 6 5 4 3 2 1

OPM

To my dear *sister* Lauren

Contents

1

Identical?

Mallie Graber sat in the schoolyard under the shade of a sycamore tree. She had picked a pile of dandelion flowers and was braiding them into a crown. The sun blazed. Mallie's flowers hung limp in her hands. Across the yard, the air above the school's war garden seemed to shimmer. The potato plants and cabbages lay covered in brown dust. Mallie knew they were not dying. She had helped water them only that morning. But they looked like they were dying.

Mallie felt like a wilted cabbage. Her stockings and shoes were smothering her, and so was her wool school dress. She wished someone would pour a bucket of water over her head. In three days school would be over. Mallie couldn't wait.

"Mallie! Hey, Mallie! Come play with us!"

Mallie looked up. Her sister, Hallie, and their friend Ruthie waved. Ruthie held up a jump rope.

"It's too hot," Mallie said.

"Mallie!" Hallie marched across the yard, Ruthie right behind. "We need a third person. Come on."

Mallie leaned against the trunk of the tree. "It's too hot," she said. She tied the ends of her crown together and twirled it in her hands.

Hallie sighed. "It's not hot. There are only ten minutes of recess left. We finally got the jump rope away from Alice."

Mallie didn't move. Hallie nudged her with a foot. "It's not hot."

"It is for me," Mallie said. "Get someone else." She put the crown of flowers on her head.

"But we want you," Ruthie said.

"Sit down," Mallie offered. "There's plenty of room in the shade."

Ruthie sat. "I'm so hot I could die."

Mallie patted her crown into place. Like Ruthie and Hallie, she wore her hair in two long braids, with ribbons tied in bows on the ends. Mallie had three sets of hair ribbons. Some of the other girls had six or even seven sets. Ruthie had four. Sometimes Hallie or Mallie switched with her on the way to school so it looked like they all had more.

Hallie never switched with Mallie, of course, because their ribbons were exactly alike. Their stockings, shoes, skirts, blouses, and dresses were all exactly alike. Even their underwear was the same.

Their faces were exactly the same. Their smiles, side by side, looked exactly alike. Their eyes were the same color and their ears the same shape. Mallie and Hallie were identical twins—the only twins in Cedarville, the only twins they knew. Except for the front tooth Hallie had chipped two years earlier falling off a seesaw, there was no way, looking at them, to tell them apart.

Hallie snorted. "You look silly in that crown," she said. "Flower chains are for babies. You're ten years old. Fourth-graders who are almost fifth-graders don't play with dandelions."

"Piffle," Mallie said. "This one does." She jammed another flower into the front of her crown so that it hung over her forehead like the forelock of a horse. She bobbed her head. The flower danced. "That's better."

Hallie snatched the flower out and flung it away. "Jump rope with us!" she said.

"Don't be rude," Ruthie told Hallie. She got to her feet. "Please. We need three people," she said to Mallie.

Mallie heaved a great sigh and stood up. "First you have to apologize," she told Hallie.

"I'm sorry," Hallie said.

"And give me my flower back."

Hallie rolled her eyes, but she plucked the dandelion out of the dirt and stuffed it into Mallie's crown. Mallie shook her head to make sure it felt right. "Okay," she said. "I'll play."

"I just hope nobody thinks I'm you," Hallie said. She handed Mallie one end of the rope.

"Keep your mouth open, then."

To Mallie's disgust, Hallie did. She jumped rope with her teeth bared like a tiger's so that everyone could see her broken tooth.

Mallie didn't think that tooth was something Hallie should display. Still, she guessed she understood. When her turn came to jump, she held on to her crown with one hand. However much Hallie wanted to be different from her, it was only a tenth as much as she wanted to be different from Hallie. Mallie would have given a thousand dollars in gold not to be a twin.

2

One Poem for Two

The bell rang. The pupils trailed inside. Miss Lane, the schoolteacher, sat at her desk and wiped her forehead with her handkerchief. Inside was hotter than outside. Every window was open, but there was no breeze. Mallie felt sweat trickle along her scalp beneath her crown.

"Hallie." Miss Lane spoke softly. Mallie looked up. Miss Lane nodded at Mallie's head.

"I'm Mallie," Mallie whispered.

"Mallie," Miss Lane corrected herself. "Put the flowers away, please."

Mallie got up and dumped them into her lunch pail. Miss Lane always confused her with Hallie. Mr. Ames, their old teacher, never had. He was in the navy now.

"Thank you," Miss Lane said. She began to call pupils forward. They all had poems to memorize for the school picnic on Saturday.

Hallie squirmed in her seat. "I told you," she said.

Mallie gave her an evil look. "It wasn't because the flowers were babyish."

"But they were," Hallie said. Mallie stuck out her tongue.

"Hallie and Mallie." For a moment Mallie thought they were in trouble, but it was just their turn to recite. She followed Hallie to the front of the classroom.

Miss Lane smiled. "Let's hear how you two are coming along," she said.

Suddenly Mallie's blood boiled over. "Why 'you two'?" she said. "Why not 'you' and 'you,' separate? Why didn't we get our own poems?"

Miss Lane had assigned them a single long poem, "The Wreck of the *Hesperus,*" to say together. It was a thrilling piece about a shipwreck. Until that moment, Mallie had loved it.

"Everyone else got their own poem," Mallie went on. "I don't want to recite with Hallie. I want my own poem." She looked at Hallie. "Don't you?"

"No," Hallie said. "I like saying it with you."

"Well, I don't." Mallie realized the other students were staring. She dropped her voice. "May I have my own poem, please?"

Miss Lane shook her head. "You should have asked three weeks ago. The picnic is on Saturday, Mallie. You can't learn a new poem in three days."

"Yes, I can." Mallie stubbed her foot against a raised plank in the floor.

"*I* can't!" Hallie crossed her arms. "I don't want to, either."

Miss Lane nodded. "I'm sorry, Mallie. I wish you'd told me your feelings before. Next year you may have your own poem. Let me hear 'The Wreck of the *Hesperus*' now."

Mallie felt her chin quiver. "Mr. Ames would have given me my own poem," she said.

She heard Hallie hiss in disbelief. She heard one of the older pupils laugh.

Miss Lane frowned, but she didn't look angry. She never did. Miss Lane didn't care how they felt about her; she didn't love teaching the way Mr. Ames had. She did it because it was her duty in this time of war.

"You'll have to write me an essay," she said.

"One hundred words, due tomorrow, on the subject of impertinence."

"Yes, ma'am," Mallie said, looking at the floor. Hallie took a step closer. Mallie stepped away.

When school let out, all the girls walked down the street together. Cedarville was too small to have its own Red Cross chapter, but it had a knitting circle that met every Wednesday afternoon for two hours. All the women in town, and all the girls down to the first-graders, belonged. They knit things for the brave soldiers fighting overseas. So far Mallie alone had made thirteen washcloths, twenty pairs of stockings, a sweater, and three mufflers; Hallie had matched her. It was all plain knitting of the most boring sort. It was their duty to do it.

The grown women went to Red Cross meetings in Leo and Fort Wayne as well. They made bandages and raised money for war relief. In the evenings, Miss Lane taught nursing classes at the Red Cross.

"Mallie Graber," said Maude, an older girl Mallie detested, "I never heard anyone sass a teacher like you." She swished her skirt in front of Mallie. "Your mother will be ashamed."

Mallie bit her lip.

"Won't she?" Maude persisted.

Mallie still didn't say anything.

"Are *you* going to tell her, Maude?" Ruthie asked. "I should have known you'd snitch."

Maude tossed her head. "I just feel sorry for *Hallie.* To have a sister like that."

Mallie looked at Hallie. To her surprise, Hallie looked away. She hunched her shoulders and walked faster.

Mallie turned to Ruthie. "What's wrong with Hallie?"

Ruthie looked uncomfortable. "You told the whole school you didn't want to say a poem with her."

"I didn't mean it that way. I just wanted my own poem."

Ruthie shrugged. "Same thing."

"No, it isn't." Mallie swung her knitting bag in frustration.

Ruthie pointed across the street. "There're our mothers," she said. Mrs. Hawk and Mrs. Graber were pushing their baby carriages out of McClennan's general store. Mallie's little sister,

Sarah, and Ruthie's littlest brother, Bert, were both almost two years old.

"Mallie!" Sarah saw Mallie and waved. Mallie ran across the street and buried her face in Sarah's hair. She breathed in Sarah's sweet smell.

Mallie's mother kissed her. "How was school?"

Mallie piled her knitting bag and books into the carriage beside Sarah and pushed it along the sidewalk. "Not too good," she said at last.

"I know it's hard to sit still and learn in this heat," Mrs. Graber said. "Perhaps Mrs. Ellis will have lemonade for us."

Mrs. Ellis, a widow with no children, was hosting the knitting circle that day. She made Mallie itch. Going to her house was not worth an entire pitcher of lemonade.

Mother squeezed Mallie's shoulder. "I expect you to be polite," she said. "Where's Hallie?"

Mallie waved her hand. "Up there. She's in a horrible mood."

Mother looked concerned. "That's not like her."

"It's not my fault," Mallie said. "I didn't do anything wrong."

3

The Mail-Order Bride

Mrs. Ellis greeted the group at the door. "Mrs. Hawk, Mrs. Graber, so glad you could come. Ruthie, good to see you, too. And here are the little Graber twins! My!" She pinched Mallie's cheek before Mallie could duck. "I don't know how your mother ever tells the two of you apart."

Mrs. Ellis always said that.

"I've got a bad tooth," Hallie said, opening her mouth wide.

Mother smiled politely. She pulled on Hallie's arm and gave Mallie a little push through the door. Mrs. Ellis blocked the way so that she could pinch Hallie's cheek, too. "My goodness, they are as alike as two peas in a pod!" She beamed at Mother. "It must be just like having the same child twice!"

Mother's smile became less polite. "Well, thank you, but I never—"

"Whenever I see one I see the other, too, and they're always dressed exactly alike! So charming!"

"Perhaps I can take Sarah—"

"The babies can play in the side yard," Mrs. Ellis said.

"I'll do that!" Hallie said. She grabbed Sarah and Bert and escaped.

Good riddance, thought Mallie.

Mrs. Ellis ushered them into her parlor. The women took the chairs and the girls sat on the floor. Mallie heard Maude laugh at her as she came in. She sat down near the door as far away from Maude as possible. Ruthie slumped beside her.

"Look at this child," Mrs. Ellis said, pointing at Mallie. "I want you ladies to guess. Which twin is it? I can't tell."

Maude giggled, but no one else said anything. Mother laid her hand against Mallie's shoulder. "Please don't tease her," she said to

Mrs. Ellis. Mallie leaned hard against Mother's knee.

"Which one are you, dearie?" Mrs. Ellis persisted. "You'll have to tell me, otherwise I might guess wrong."

"That's Mallie," Maude said. "You can tell because she's been sulking all day."

Mallie took a half-finished muffler from her bag and began to knit. Her hands shook. She dropped a stitch. She picked it up, concentrating hard. She was glad when Mrs. Hendricks, the chair of the knitting circle, called them to order.

"As usual, we have not been able to get khaki yarn," Mrs. Hendricks said. "The Supply Bureau has again provided us with gray, which is still acceptable. Our goal this week is stockings. . . ."

Mallie looked out the window. Hallie, Sarah, and Bert were running in circles in the tiny patch of grass left over beside Mrs. Ellis's big war garden. Hallie was laughing.

Mallie took her spare pair of knitting needles from her bag and dug their tips into Mrs. Ellis's carpet. They stood up straight by themselves. When Ruthie pulled one out and scratched her back with it, Ruthie's mother took it away from her and raised her eyebrows at Mallie. Mallie plucked the remaining needle out of the carpet. Mother patted Mallie's shoulder again.

Mrs. Hendricks began passing out hanks of gray wool. Everything they knit was made of gray wool, except the washcloths and bed socks, which were white cotton. Mallie knew that made sense; bright colors were cheerful but easy to shoot at. Soldiers were better off dull.

Mallie pulled at the front of her tight, scratchy dress. The air in the parlor was stifling. She worked on her muffler—one row, then another. The women talked above the click of their needles. Mallie wished Mrs. Ellis would give them lemonade and let them all go home.

"I cannot imagine how that poor bride felt when she got off the train and found herself standing next to squint-eyed Josiah Jenkins," Mrs. Ellis was saying. "I quite pity the child."

Mallie looked up, startled. Mr. Jenkins was their neighbor. He was a good farmer. He couldn't see well enough to join the army or navy, but he served in the Home Guard.

"Bride?" Ruthie whispered. Mallie nodded. She'd heard that word, too. Mr. Jenkins was a

bachelor. He was an old man. Mallie guessed he was thirty at least.

Mother cleared her throat. "I wouldn't call Mr. Jenkins squint-eyed," she said. "He is a kind man and a hard worker, and his eyesight is no fault of his own. He keeps his farm well. His cherry trees are beautiful."

"We must remember our audience," Ruthie's mother added. "Young girls—"

"But it's unimaginable!" Mrs. Ellis cut back in. "A mail-order bride here in Cedarville! And a New Englander, to boot!"

"What's a mail-order bride?" asked Ruthie.

There was silence. The women in the room looked at each other.

"You can't get a wife from Sears Roebuck, can you?" Ruthie continued. "I mean, I know you can get *pigs*—"

Miss Lane laughed. She had come late after closing up the school. "You can advertise for a wife in the classified sections of some newspapers," she said. "Mr. Jenkins did that. He didn't tell anyone until today, after they were married."

"Which newspaper did he use?" asked Ruthie.

Miss Lane shook her head. "I didn't ask."

"Boston," Mrs. Ellis said. "She's from Boston."

Mallie wondered how Mrs. Ellis knew. The way she said "Boston," it sounded like a bad place. Mallie looked at her mother. "Is it shameful?" she asked.

"Mail-order brides are not common around here," Mother said. "But there is no shame in marrying Mr. Jenkins. He is a good man."

Mrs. Hendricks sat back in her chair. "There may be shame in marrying *Mrs.* Jenkins," she announced. "I called upon her this afternoon, as soon as I learned of her arrival." Mrs. Hendricks's voice rose. "She has refused to join the Red Cross. She says she wants nothing to do with the war."

Nothing to do with the war! A shocked hiss traveled the room. Mallie dropped her knitting. It was like saying you didn't believe in God.

"Yes," Mrs. Hendricks said. "I tried to explain that we needed every hand . . . our brave boys in France . . ." Her voice faltered. She closed her mouth and shook her head. Mrs. Hendricks's two sons were fighting in France. They had enlisted the same week war was declared.

So had most of the young men in Cedarville. Allen County, Indiana, had led the entire nation in enlistments. Everyone was proud of that.

Mallie looked around the room. All the women seemed upset. How could Mr. Jenkins's new wife be so unfeeling? Mallie picked up her needles and knit with new energy. Next winter her muffler would keep a soldier warm.

Ruthie leaned over. "How could she marry someone she'd never met?"

"I don't know." Mallie thought about it. Either Mrs. Jenkins was brave or she was foolhardy.

Maybe both, Mallie decided. Brave *and* foolhardy. She smiled at Ruthie. "I would do it. I would be a mail-order bride."

4

Gypsies

"I want to be called Matilda," Mallie said on the way home. Mother and Mrs. Hawk were far ahead, discussing Mrs. Jenkins. Hallie, Mallie, and Ruthie walked side by side. Their farms were next to each other just outside Cedarville.

"You're starting again," Hallie said. "Stop it."

"*You* didn't have to talk to Mrs. Ellis," Mallie said. "Miss Lane didn't call *you* by the wrong name. I'm tired of being called Hallie. I'm tired of being called Mallie. I'm tired of always being second."

"You're not second," Hallie said.

"Say our names," Mallie shot back.

"Hallie and Mallie."

"See! I'm *And Mallie.* I'm not even second, I'm the second half! I hate it!"

Hallie looked stricken. "You're not And Mallie," she said. "You're Mallie."

"Then why doesn't anyone ever say, 'Here's Mallie and Hallie'? Why do they always say, 'Hallie and Mallie'?"

" 'Mallie and Hallie' sounds funny," Hallie said. "It's not my fault."

"I don't care," Mallie said. "I want to be called Matilda from now on, always." She looked at Ruthie. "Okay?"

Ruthie sniffed. "I wish I had a twin sister." She put her arm around Hallie. "I wouldn't mind being called And Ruthie." Ruthie had six brothers and no sisters.

"Then I'll call you And Ruthie," Mallie said. She kicked a stone in the road.

They were almost to the Hawks' lane when they heard a shout. "Mother! Ruthie! Mother!"

Ruthie looked up. "It's Paul," she said.

Paul was Ruthie's next-oldest brother, the oldest still at home. He burst onto the road. "Mother!" Ruthie's four-year-old brother, Charlie, ran after him, sobbing.

Mrs. Hawk reached for Charlie. "What's wrong?"

"The Gypsies are here!" Paul said. He shook his hair out of his eyes and laughed. "Mother, the Gypsies have come."

"Is that all?" said Mrs. Hawk. She wiped Charlie's face.

"Gypsies?" asked Mrs. Graber.

Mrs. Hawk nodded. "They come through town every year, right about this time."

"Remember?" Hallie said. "We had chicken pox last year when they came. We didn't see them."

Mother nodded. "That's right. With all three of you ill, and Sarah so sick, I don't think I left the house for three weeks."

Before that, Hallie and Mallie had lived in Harlan. Mallie had never seen a Gypsy, but she knew what one was. The Gypsies had come from Europe long ago. They didn't have homes. They drove bright wagons and camped wherever they went. Now they were here, in Cedarville. Mallie's stomach gave an excited lurch.

Charlie burst into tears again. "I'm scared of the Gypsies," he said.

"There's nothing to be afraid of," his mother told him.

"The Gypsies will eat me!" Charlie howled. "Ted said!"

Ted was Ruthie's second-oldest brother. He and Joe, the oldest, were in Philadelphia, working in a factory making guns for the war. Joe had been gone for over a year. Ted had left only a month ago. He was fifteen. He had wanted to be part of the war effort. Mallie figured he had also wanted to be in Philadelphia. Ted liked excitement.

"The Gypsies won't eat you," Mrs. Hawk said. "Your father bought a horse from them once. He wouldn't buy a horse from someone who was going to eat you."

"They're nasty, dirty thieves," Ruthie said, "but they won't eat you."

"Ruthie, please," said Mrs. Hawk. She looked at Paul. "Are they camping on the creek bottom?"

Paul nodded. "Father said they could."

Mrs. Hawk looked at Mallie's mother. "He always lets them camp on our land. He thinks they're less likely to steal from us if he does. I still seem to lose half a dozen good hens a year."

"Gypsies are thieves," Ruthie said.

"Ruthie hates them," Paul said. "Gypsy girls ride horses, you know."

Mallie nodded. Ruthie's brothers all rode the farm horses sometimes. Ruthie couldn't, because she was a girl.

"Should I be worried?" Mrs. Graber asked Mrs. Hawk. "If they're camping by the creek, they're as close to my house as yours."

Mrs. Hawk shook her head. "They won't do more than steal hens or a sack of grain," she said. "I doubt you'll even catch them at that."

"Can we play with them?" Mallie asked.

"Mallie, no!" Mother said sharply.

"They're scandalous," Ruthie said. "They wear low-cut blouses. They hardly wear underwear. And all bright colors—red, orange, everything."

"Just stay away from them," Mrs. Hawk said. "They'll move on soon enough."

Mallie looked at the dull green plaid of her school dress. She'd never wanted a scandalous blouse before. But wouldn't Hallie's eyes pop if she wore one! She would certainly look different from Hallie then. Mallie laughed.

"And," Paul said, puffing his chest importantly, "Mr. Jenkins has ordered himself a wife!"

"Oh, Paul," Ruthie said, "we already know all about that."

Mallie barely heard Ruthie say good-bye. She couldn't wait to see the Gypsies. They sounded interesting. Exciting. *Different*. Mallie knew that none of the Gypsy girls—if indeed there were Gypsy girls—would be twins.

5

Mother's Surprise

As soon as the Hawks were out of ear-shot, Mother stopped and turned to Hallie and Mallie. "I want the two of you to know something," she said. "Mrs. Ellis and the rest of the townsfolk might think you look exactly alike, but I don't. I have been able to tell you apart since the moment you were born."

A feeling of relief hit Mallie with the suddenness of a summer storm. "That's right," she said, looking at her mother. "You always know."

Mallie had never realized it before. When she walked into the kitchen in the morning, Mother always said, "Good morning, Mallie," right away. Sarah and Father sometimes got them confused, but Mother never did.

"How can you tell?" she asked.

Mother thought for a moment. "Your ears are a little different, and the expressions in your eyes," she answered. "And Hallie's hairline dips lower."

"And my tooth," Hallie said.

"But you only broke it a few years ago," Mother pointed out. She shook her head. "Mrs. Ellis has never bothered me much before, but today I wanted to give her a piece of my mind. The way she goes on about the two of you! As though a single pair of twins were the eighth wonder of the world."

"Most people are like her," Mallie said. "They think we're the same because we look the same. And they think I'm second."

"Don't be silly," Mother said. "No one thinks you're second."

"Please, will you call me Matilda?" Mallie asked.

"*I* won't," Hallie said.

Mother looked at them. "Don't argue," she said. She adjusted the hood of the carriage to shade Sarah's face. Sarah had fallen asleep.

"Please?" Mallie asked. Mother didn't say anything. They turned down their lane.

"Where's Father?" Hallie asked. The barn door was open and the wagon was gone.

"He took pigs into town," said Mother. Mr. Graber farmed sheep and hogs, as well as wheat and corn. Because of the war, he was raising more animals and crops than ever. The soldiers needed food. Father was always tired.

In the kitchen Mallie lifted the wet cloth off the pitcher of milk on the counter. She poured a glass and took a sip. She shuddered. The cloth helped keep the pitcher cold, but it hadn't kept it cold enough.

Mother noticed. "Is that milk sour already?"

Mallie nodded. Mother sighed. "It was fresh this morning." She shook her head. "There's no keeping food in this heat. I don't know what we'll have for supper. I don't want to build a fire in the stove. If this kitchen gets any hotter we'll roast."

Mallie rinsed her glass and filled it with water. The water was warm.

"We need an icebox," Hallie said. "Maude has one."

"Maude lives in town," Mother said. "Your father can't drive in every day just for a block of ice."

"Are you going to visit Mr. Jenkins's wife?" asked Mallie.

Mother nodded. "After the picnic, when I have more time. I'm sorry she already upset Mrs. Hendricks. I hope she'll try to fit in. If she won't support the war effort, it will be hard for her to live here."

"Maybe she doesn't care," Mallie said. "Maybe she likes to be different."

Mother looked at her. "Mallie, she'll be lonely without friends."

"Please call me Matilda."

"Matilda, dear," Mother said, "is it really so important?"

Mallie nodded.

"Not to me," Hallie said. "You can call me anything you want."

"*And* Hallie," Mallie muttered.

"What's that?" asked Mother.

"Do you really think we're different?" Mallie asked.

"Of course," Mother said. She began taking dishes from the cupboard, then suddenly stopped and shook her head. "How could I forget?" she said. "With all the excitement today, I haven't told you—"

She was interrupted by a shout from outside. "Elizabeth!" They jumped up. It was Father.

Father had driven the wagon right to the front of the house. There was a huge square shape covered with horse blankets in the back. "A little surprise," Father said. "It's for Mother."

"Is it an icebox?" Hallie guessed.

Mallie looked at it. If it was an icebox, it was the biggest one she'd ever seen. She brushed her hands against her skirt and walked up to the horses. They were lathered and blowing. "It must be heavy," Mallie said, looking up at Father. "The horses had trouble pulling it."

"It is heavy," Father said. He looked at Mother, who stood on the porch holding Sarah. "Can't you guess?" he asked. He was smiling from ear to ear, the way he did in winter when he wasn't so tired. He was smiling his Christmas-morning smile.

Mother let Sarah slide to the ground. She put her hand to her mouth. Her eyes shone. Father pulled the blankets away. Mother gave a little cry of joy. The surprise was a piano.

"A piano?" said Hallie. "We needed an icebox."

Mallie shrugged. Father helped Mother into

the wagon, and Mother kissed him right in front of them. "Mother wanted one," Mallie whispered.

"Why?" asked Hallie.

Mallie shook her head. She didn't know.

The piano was too heavy for Father to unload by himself. "I'll get help tomorrow," he promised. He drove the wagon into the barn and unhitched the team.

Mother rode into the barn on the piano bench while Hallie and Mallie followed, pulling Sarah along between them. Mother opened the cover over the piano keys and began to play notes one at a time.

"Is that a song?" Mallie asked.

Mother laughed. "No, I'm just listening," she said. "It's held its tune well."

"Knocked around a bit on the trip," Father said.

"It's beautiful," Mother said.

"Secondhand," said Father.

"Perfect," said Mother.

Hallie grabbed Mallie's arm. "Let's pick some vegetables," she said. "Otherwise we'll never get supper."

Mallie looked back over her shoulder at her parents. She hadn't known Mother wanted a piano. She hadn't even known Mother could play the piano. It made her feel like she didn't know Mother very well at all.

"Do you think we'll get to play, too?" she asked Hallie.

"I hope not," Hallie said. She grabbed a handful of peas. "What do you think?"

Mallie searched for a ripe tomato. "Just because you don't want to, doesn't mean I don't want to."

"Well, I know *that.*" Hallie turned her face away. "I was there when you told the whole school you didn't want to recite a poem with me."

Mallie sighed. "I didn't mean to tell the whole school," she said. "Besides, you feel the same way. You jumped rope with your mouth open!"

"You had flowers on your head! When you act like a normal person, I'm not ashamed of you."

"I'm not ashamed of you," Mallie said.

Hallie shook her head and stomped back

toward the house. Mallie watched her go. She couldn't decide whether she felt sad or angry.

"Hallie and Mallie!" Mother called from the porch.

And Mallie again. Mallie dragged her feet through the grass. She felt sad and angry both.

6

Different

Supper was so confusing, Mallie could barely eat. Father was full of the story of how he'd come to trade three young pigs for a secondhand piano. Mother hung on every word.

"Mallie made such a fuss in school today," Hallie said. Mallie glared at her. Hallie glared back.

"I did not," Mallie said.

"That's good," said Mother. "I'll have to find my music books. I think they're in the trunk upstairs."

"She has to write an essay on impertinence," Hallie said. "It's because she didn't want to say our poem."

"Please be quiet," Mallie said through her teeth.

"More!" Sarah shouted, banging the edge of her high chair. Mother piled another spoonful of peas onto Sarah's plate.

"I knew how happy you'd be," Father said, leaning back in his chair with a smile. "How long has it been since you last played? Thirteen years?"

"Fourteen," Mother said. "Since we've been married." She smiled at Hallie and Mallie. "I'll teach you girls to play."

"She was really rude," Hallie said, more loudly.

"I was not!" said Mallie.

Suddenly Mother and Father paid attention. "Why not?" asked Father.

Mallie was startled. "Why not what?" she said.

"That's what I'm asking," Father said. "What were you?"

"Rude," Hallie said.

"Was not!" yelled Mallie.

Father raised his eyebrows. "Explain," he said, pointing to Hallie.

Hallie told her side of the story. "Miss Lane

said it was too late," she finished. "We have to say our poem together."

"Well, then, it's settled," Father said.

"But it was embarrassing," Hallie said, shooting a mean glance at Mallie. "She has to write an essay."

"I'll write it," said Mallie.

Mother still looked radiant. "Speaking of the picnic," she said, "I still haven't told you my surprise. Today I cut new Sunday dresses for you girls. I've basted them, and you can try them on tonight. If we all hurry, we can get them finished for you to wear on Saturday. I think you'll really like them. I've made them different this time."

"New dresses!" Mallie was indeed surprised. They had fewer new clothes than ever, because of the war. Soldiers needed uniforms. Fabric was hard to get, and expensive.

Mother laughed. "You had to have them," she said. "You've worn your old summer dresses for three years."

"How are they different?" Hallie asked. Mallie noticed that Hallie's eyes were shining.

Mother smiled. "You'll see."

Mallie's heart began to beat faster. Different!

It would be wonderful to have a dress that wasn't exactly like Hallie's. Maybe hers would be a different style, or maybe it would be a different color. Mallie didn't care. Different was different.

After supper, Mother took them upstairs to her bedroom. White lawn fabric covered the bed. "Look," Mother said, picking up a dress and shaking it out. "Sailor style! Aren't they nice?"

Mallie looked. She saw not two but *three* identical dresses—two larger ones, and one very small one. She swallowed hard. She couldn't believe it. Sarah was going to dress like them, too.

"You said they were different," Mallie said.

"They are," Mother said. "You've never had sailor dresses before." She frowned. "Don't you like them?"

Mallie bit her lip. She blinked back tears. Hallie took a deep breath, then walked forward and threw her arms around Mother. "They're beautiful," she said. "Thank you for making us new dresses."

Mallie made herself think of her old summer

dress. She remembered how tight it felt under her arms. She remembered how thin and faded it was. She closed her eyes and tried to act like Hallie. "Thank you," she whispered. But she had a bitter heart.

7

The Red Blouse

On the way to school the next morning, they saw the Gypsy camp.

A thunderstorm in the night had cleared away the heat. The morning breeze smelled fresh and cool, and the lane felt firm beneath their feet. Mallie had dreamed of white dresses, hundreds of them, all in a row, all alike. In the morning her own white dress was still there. Mallie dreaded wearing it.

Around a bend in the road, Mallie saw smoke from a campfire. She heard someone singing. "Look!" she said to Hallie.

"It's just Granny Watkins frying trout for breakfast," Hallie said. Old Mrs. Watkins often fished early.

"No," Mallie said, "it's the Gypsies."

They pushed through the brush at the edge of the road. The land dipped low along the bank of the river, and there, under the shelter of the trees, the Gypsies had set up camp. Three brightly painted covered wagons stood close to one another. Horses grazed on a line nearby. An old, plump Gypsy woman held her long skirts out of the way as she hung a pot over the campfire. Her hair hung down in two long silver braids. She had her back to them, but Mallie could hear her singing.

Hallie sniffed. "Imagine living in a wagon."

Mallie thought the camp looked cozy. She stepped out of the weeds.

Hallie grabbed her arm. "Where are you going?"

Mallie shook free. "I'm going to say good morning," she said. "Like I'd do for Granny Watkins."

"She's not Granny Watkins!" Hallie held her back.

"Why shouldn't I?" Mallie asked. She watched the Gypsy stir her stew pot. "Ruthie *said* they don't eat people." When Hallie didn't smile, Mallie added, "They won't hurt me."

"I'll tell Father," Hallie said. "We'll be late for school."

Mallie sighed. "Okay," she said, stepping back into the brush.

Just then a girl poked her head out of one of the wagons. She climbed over the seat and hopped to the ground. A real Gypsy girl! She looked just the same age as Mallie. Mallie watched her run barefoot across the grass. Her loose black hair swung over her shoulders, down to her waist. She wore a flowered skirt and had bracelets on her arms. Her blouse was the most brilliant shade of red Mallie had ever seen.

"Oh!" Mallie caught her breath.

The girl ran up to the old woman and said something in a language Mallie didn't understand.

"Look at her hair," Mallie whispered. "Look at that blouse."

"They're strange," Hallie whispered back. "Let's get away before they see us." She pulled Mallie up the embankment.

Mallie looked back again and again to admire the girl's scarlet blouse and black hair. Just as she reached the top the old Gypsy woman turned around. She met Mallie's gaze and nodded once. Mallie nodded back.

"The old woman knew we were there," she said as they started walking down the road again.

Hallie shuddered. She waved to Ruthie, who was waiting for them at the top of her lane. "We saw the Gypsies!" she called.

"There aren't as many this year as last," Ruthie said. "I spied on them from the orchard. Father won't let me go close."

"They're probably in the army like everyone else," said Hallie.

"Maybe," Ruthie said. "Or if they're not, the men are smart enough not to parade around town."

"They were *beautiful,*" Mallie burst out. "The wagons were so neat, and the horses so graceful—and that girl in the red blouse, she looked so happy." Mallie thought with envy of the Gypsy girl's bare feet. No scratchy stockings for her. No shared poems, either, and certainly no matching sailor dresses.

Ruthie and Hallie stared at her as though she were speaking Chinese. "We shouldn't have stopped," Hallie said.

"They looked nice," Mallie insisted.

Ruthie swung her lunch pail. "I bet they looked well fed. I only found forty eggs in our henhouse this morning. You can't tell me that pack of Gypsies isn't eating eggs today."

"I didn't smell eggs," Mallie said.

Ruthie laughed. "Don't take up for them, Mallie. Gypsies aren't like us."

Mallie looked her in the eye. "I know," she said. "That's why I like them."

8

And Matilda

"Ignore her," Hallie said. "She's still in a bad mood from yesterday."

"Let's do a ribbon swap," said Ruthie.

She and Hallie put down their books. Mallie kept walking. A few minutes later Hallie and Ruthie skipped past her wearing each other's hair ribbons. Mallie smiled. She didn't look exactly like Hallie now.

"Hey, Ruthie," she called. Ruthie stopped and waited for her. "Will you do a swap with me?"

"What for?" Ruthie said. "You'd be wearing Hallie's ribbons."

"Not ribbons." Mallie's idea was so good, she wondered why she hadn't thought of it before. "Swap your poem with me. I'll say yours, and you can recite mine with Hallie. Then Hallie won't have to learn a new one. She won't mind. Miss Lane won't mind. Please."

Ruthie bit her lip. "I'd have to learn a new poem," she said.

"It's so easy. I'll help you."

Ruthie looked doubtful.

"I'll give you my ribbons," Mallie said. "For keeps. The ones I'm wearing now."

"No." Ruthie shook her head. "My mother would make me give them back. And I like my poem, and Hallie would be mad. I don't want to."

"Please! I'd do it for you!" Mallie wanted to stamp her feet.

"No," Ruthie said. "You shouldn't ask me to do something that would upset Hallie."

Mallie huffed past her. She stomped into the schoolyard, up the steps, and into the school. Miss Lane was sitting at her desk. "Miss Lane?"

The teacher looked up from her book. "Yes, Hallie?"

"I'm *Mallie.* Only I don't wish to be called Mallie anymore. From now on, please address me by my given name."

Miss Lane nodded. "Certainly."

"Thank you." Mallie turned on her heel to go out.

"There's just one thing . . ."

"Yes?" Mallie turned back around.

Miss Lane smiled. "What *is* your given name?"

"Matilda," Mallie said. "Matilda Marie Graber. It does *not* rhyme with Hallie."

Miss Lane called the fourth grade forward by names as usual. "Ruth Hawk," she said. Then she made a point of looking at Mallie. "Hallie and *Matilda* Graber."

And Matilda. It was not an improvement at all. Mallie marched to the front of the room. Her insides boiled. She was going to have to do something soon.

9

Straight Seams

At home Mother was sewing in the parlor. Pieces of their dresses lay across the top of the new piano. Sarah had fallen asleep on a heap of fabric in the corner. "I've nearly finished the bodices," Mother said, smiling. "I'll work on Sarah's dress now. You two can sew your skirts. Go carefully so the seams are straight."

Mallie took the skirt Mother gave her and pinned it to her dress above her knee. She pulled it tight across her lap. She didn't care whether her seams were straight or not, since she roundly hated her dress. She felt like sewing crookedly on purpose. Mother would make her pick the seams out and start over, and with any luck the dress wouldn't be finished in time for the picnic.

But then she would have nothing to wear at all. She would look ridiculous in her old summer dress. Mallie pursed her mouth and began to sew.

Mother kept looking at the piano. "I've been in such a rush with these dresses, I haven't had time to play more than a few scales," she said. "Next week we'll start your lessons. Won't that be fun?"

"Of course," Hallie answered. Hallie always said the right thing.

"Mallie?"

Mallie looked up. She was angry enough to say no. Only she really did want to play the piano. She could imagine its keys cool beneath her fingertips. "Of course," she said, but she rolled her eyes. She didn't want Mother to think she was too happy. Mother frowned.

"Did you hear any more about the Sears Roebuck wife?" Hallie asked. "I mean, the mail-order bride?"

Mother laughed. "It's not polite to mention how Mrs. Jenkins came here," she said. "But no,

I haven't heard any news. I haven't been out of the house today."

"We saw the Gypsies," Hallie said. "Mallie liked them."

Mallie looked up. "There was a girl our age. She looked nice."

"Maude says they kidnap children," said Hallie. "She says they sell them for slaves. She says everybody knows to stay away from Gypsies." Hallie lifted her chin.

"Maude tells lies," said Mallie.

"Stay away from the Gypsies, Mallie. Even the children," Mother said. "You can't trust them. But don't worry about being kidnapped. That's just something people say. I've never heard of its being true."

Mallie nodded. She knew it was a lie. Probably the Gypsies didn't actually steal things, either. She felt sorry for them.

Mallie finished her first seam, made a new knot in her thread, and started to overcast the seam's raw edge.

"Oh, no, Mallie," Mother said. "Make French seams. Like Hallie."

"Do I have to?" Mallie asked. She held up the skirt. "I've already finished this the regular way. Nice and straight, with lots of backstitching."

Mother shook her head. "The fabric is so fine, it won't hold up in the wash. Rip out what you've done and start over, please."

"I hate this," Mallie muttered.

"Don't grumble," Mother said. "You don't want your dress to fall apart. You're lucky to have a new dress at all."

Children were starving in war-torn Europe. Soldiers were dying in battle. Mallie had food and a new dress. "I'm sorry," she said.

When Mother left the room to start supper, Mallie looked over at her twin. Hallie was already gathering the top edge of her skirt. Mallie had barely started her second French seam. "Don't worry," Hallie said. "Mother will help you. She'll make sure both our dresses are ready."

"You mean all three of them." Mallie tilted her head toward Sarah.

"Right," Hallie said. She began to stroke the gathers she'd made.

"Don't you hate it?" Mallie asked.

"Gathers? They aren't half as bad as pleats."

"No." Mallie's voice came out so angry that

she felt forced to speak low. "The matching dresses. The matching shoes and stockings and hair ribbons. Us looking as much alike with our clothes on as we would stark naked."

Hallie looked up. Her eyes were wary. "It isn't my fault I was born first," she said. "It isn't my fault everyone says 'Hallie and Mallie.' 'Mallie and Hallie' sounds awkward; I can't help that."

"Tell me one thing," Mallie said. "Do you like our dresses being the same?"

Hallie rested her hands in her lap. "I don't mind looking like you," she said. "Not as much as you mind looking like me."

"Just answer me," Mallie said.

Hallie bit her lip and looked out the window. "I don't think about clothes very often," she said.

Mallie knew that. Hallie often got in trouble for grass stains and rips caused by carelessness. Most of Hallie's clothes were patched somewhere.

"If I had a choice," Hallie said, "I would have picked that figured muslin in McClennan's window—the one with the poppies on it. But I think it was expensive. And Mother would say it wasn't suited to children."

Mallie let out her breath. "I wanted pale blue with stripes," she said. She felt better knowing that Hallie's choice didn't match hers. Mallie thought back to the Gypsy girl's wonderful blouse. Now that she'd seen it, she favored bright red over pale blue. She would give anything to have a blouse like that. Mallie picked up her needle and began to sew again. She would give her white sailor dress, for sure.

10

A Dangerous Idea

On the last day of school Miss Lane gently called Mallie Matilda. At recess Paul Hawk called her Matilda and laughed until he fell down. Ruthie and Hallie hit him and Mallie burst into angry tears. Miss Lane sent them all inside but didn't punish them further. After all, it was the final day.

Mallie sat at her desk with her head in her arms. She was ashamed of crying.

"I don't understand you," Hallie said. "You asked to be called Matilda."

"Not by Paul," Mallie said.

"You don't know what you want," said Hallie.

Mallie wiped her eyes on her sleeve. "I know," she whispered.

Hallie touched her shoulder. "If you want," she offered, "Miss Lane can introduce me tomorrow as Hannah. She can even say Matilda and Hannah."

"Thank you," Mallie said. But she knew it wouldn't make her feel any better.

As they walked home they heard violin music coming from the Gypsy camp. Mallie tried to dance, but her arms were too full of papers and her lunch pail. She set her things down on the grass and tried again. She spun around, holding her hands in front of her. "Look!" she said. "I'm a Gypsy!" She gave a little leap.

"You don't look like a Gypsy," Hallie said.

Mallie stopped. "I know," she said. She picked up her things and walked somberly on. That was what was wrong. She looked like And Mallie, the second half of Hallie. She felt like someone else—like someone different, like a Gypsy.

At home they heard strange noises coming from the parlor. Mallie thought it was supposed to be music, but it didn't sound like music. Mother was playing notes, one right after another, higher, then lower, then higher again. It sounded like someone climbing up and down a ladder.

"What's that?" Mallie asked, walking into the room. She looked over Mother's shoulder at the music book on the piano. Mallie was used to seeing music from the hymnals at church, but this book didn't have words. The pages were filled with lines and black dots. "It looks like a bunch of ants," she said.

Mother stopped. "I suppose it does," she said. "They're finger exercises. I'm trying to get my hands back into shape so that I can play." She started again.

"Ugh," said Hallie as they went upstairs to change. "See what I mean?"

Mallie pushed open their bedroom door. Mother had laid their new dresses on the bed—completely finished. Hallie picked one up and held it against her. "They're pretty," she said.

Mallie fingered the tape sewn into the collar of the other dress. Mother always embroidered an *H* or an *M* there so they could tell their clothes apart. "You've got mine," she said.

"Oh. Sorry." Hallie traded dresses, then carefully folded hers. Mallie laid hers back on the bed. She took off her shoes and stockings and wiggled her bare feet gratefully.

Hallie slipped into her play clothes. "Let's go," she said. Ruthie had invited them over.

Mallie ran her hand over her new dress. A horrible but wonderful, dangerous but exciting idea seized her all at once. Did she dare?

"Hurry up," said Hallie.

"I'm feeling tired," Mallie said. "I think I'll stay here."

Hallie looked at her closely. "Maybe you're sick," she said. "Have you been sick all week? That would explain a lot."

"Tell Ruthie I'll see her at the picnic," Mallie said.

"Okay."

Hallie left. Mallie sat very still for several minutes. She listened to her heart beating. Then she folded her new dress into a neat bundle. She tucked it under her arm and crept down the stairs and out the door.

11

Madder

This time there were several Gypsies at the camp. An old man snored in the shade with his hat over his face, a violin on the grass beside him. A boy brushed a black horse. Several small children played tag in the grass, and the girl Mallie admired was watching them, her hands on her hips. Mallie stood still for a moment. She knew Gypsies didn't eat people or kidnap them. But would they be friendly?

"Hello," she called out, stepping forward.

The boy glanced over his shoulder. The man slept on. The children stared for a moment and then went back to their game. But the girl dropped her hands and walked toward Mallie with a saucy smile.

"Hello," Mallie said. "I'm Mallie Graber. What's your name?"

The girl looked Mallie up and down. Mallie felt herself blush. She tried to look back boldly, but she couldn't meet the girl's eyes. She ended up staring at the neckline of the girl's blouse—the same red blouse from the day before. It was simply made, collarless, but not actually scandalous, Mallie decided. No one would be offended if she wore a blouse like that. Only the color made it stand out.

"So, you've come to hear your fortune," the girl said. She had a funny way of speaking, but Mallie understood.

"No," Mallie said. "Not really. I mean—" She paused. She wouldn't mind knowing her fortune—unless it told her something awful.

The Gypsy girl tilted her chin at Mallie and walked off toward the back of one of the wagons. Mallie followed. The silver-haired old Gypsy woman was sitting on the tailgate. Her bare feet dangled above the ground.

"So," she said, smiling at Mallie. "My friend from yesterday, yes?"

Mallie held out her hand politely. "I'm Mallie Graber," she said.

The old woman grabbed it. Instead of shaking it as Mallie expected, she turned it over and studied Mallie's palm. "Good hand," she said. "Very nice hand. You've got something you want to know, eh?"

"Well—" Mallie said.

The woman stopped her. "First you got to cross it," she said.

"Cross it?"

"Cross it with silver, they say. You got to pay me, dearie, if you want your fortune told. What you got in that bundle?"

Mallie remembered the dress she was carrying. She unfolded it and held it up. The Gypsy girl was a little shorter than she was. Her idea would work.

"I didn't come to hear my fortune," she said. "I came to trade clothes."

The old woman narrowed her eyes. "What kind of trade?"

Mallie swallowed. "This dress—this good lawn dress, never worn—for her . . ." She nodded at the girl. "Her blouse and skirt."

The old woman felt the fabric of Mallie's dress. She examined the hem and cuff.

"French seams," said Mallie.

The woman said something in her strange language to the girl. The girl said something back, sharp and quick. She spat on the ground.

Mallie stepped back. The woman and girl argued for a moment. The girl spat again, with impressive force. Mallie had never known a girl to spit before.

The woman turned to Mallie and shrugged. "We don't want your dress," she said.

"But—" Mallie had been sure they would take it. Her dress was so much better than the girl's, except for the color.

"Why you want her clothes, anyway? You want to be a Gypsy? You can't be, you know." The woman gave her another sharp glance. "Gypsies are born."

"I don't like my dress," Mallie said. "I want to look different."

The woman smiled. "Different like a Gypsy?"

"Red," Mallie said. "I want something red. Something that stands out."

The woman smiled. She held up a strong, bony finger. "Wait here." She went into the wagon. The Gypsy girl smiled at Mallie again and wandered away.

The old woman came back with a large cloth bundle. She sat on the ground and opened it. Inside was a collection of paper packets. Some of them looked very old. The Gypsy hunted through them, muttering to herself. Finally she plucked one out. "Here is this," she said. She held it under Mallie's nose. "Madder. It makes a red dye. Turn your white dress Gypsy red."

Mallie's mouth fell open. That would be perfect. "I can have it?"

The Gypsy moved it out of reach. "For a price, sure."

"But I don't have any money," Mallie said.

"What you got?"

Mallie thought. She couldn't give the dress away if she was going to dye it. She couldn't give away the dress she was wearing—or could she? She held out her skirt. "This," she said. "I'll put my white dress on."

The old woman fingered Mallie's school dress. "Okay." She opened the paper packet and tipped a little of its contents onto another piece of paper. She twisted it shut. "Enough for one dress," she said.

Mallie ducked behind the wagon and changed as quickly as she could. Her new dress fit beautifully. She thrust her old dress into the Gypsy's arms, grabbed the paper packet, and ran all the way home.

12

Disaster

Mallie hid Mother's old tin washtub behind the peony bushes in the side yard. She pumped water from the well and poured two buckets of it into the tub. She added the Gypsy dye and stirred it with a stick. Some of the powder dissolved, but most settled onto the bottom of the tub. Mallie stirred again. She pulled off her white dress and dropped it into the tub. She poked the dress with the stick until it was wet through.

Mallie held her breath. How long until her dress turned that glorious Gypsy color? She'd forgotten to ask. She lifted one sleeve out of the bath. So far it was only a streaky, muddy color, a few shades darker than white. Not red. Mallie sighed. She hated to wait. After a few more minutes she sneaked into the house and put an old calico dress on over her petticoat. Hallie might be home soon.

At dinner Mother asked how they liked the new dresses. "They're beautiful, Mother," Hallie said. She passed the bowl of greens to Mallie.

Mallie's throat felt tight. Her dress had darkened, but it wasn't really red. There was something funny about the dye, too. It seemed to be settling on the fabric in blotches. "I put it on," she said softly. "It was comfortable."

"Good," Mother said.

Mallie forced a smile. Her dress would be fine. She was pretty sure it would be fine.

The dress was not red by bedtime. Mallie didn't know what to do. She needed to hang it up to dry. She almost wished she'd waited until after the picnic to dye it. She pulled it out of the washtub, then dropped it back in. She could iron it dry in the morning, when it was red. If it was red. What if it wasn't?

Mallie couldn't sleep. She tossed and turned.

"Stop moving," Hallie mumbled. Mallie held so still she could hardly breathe. But she didn't sleep. As soon as the bedroom began to grow light, she eased away from Hallie and tiptoed down the stairs.

In the garden she plunged her hands into the cold dark water. She pulled out her dress and held it up to the pale sunlight. It was ruined. The dress was brown, a funny red-green brown like the manure tea Father made to fertilize the garden. Dark streaks and stains ran across the skirt and sleeves, and a particularly ugly spot marred the center of the bodice.

Mallie was too upset to cry. She laid the dress on the damp grass and carefully emptied the washtub. There must be something she could do. Some of the dye had splashed onto her white nightgown. She scrubbed at it with her fingers before realizing that her hands were dyed, too. She couldn't escape it.

Mallie carried the washtub to the pump by the barn, then went back for her poor dress. She filled the tub with fresh, clear water and rinsed the dress over and over again. The color lightened, but not enough. Whatever the Gypsy woman had given her—mad? madden?—must have been some sort of dye at least. It hadn't stuck to the dress evenly, but it had stuck.

Mallie stood over the tub and sobbed. She wasn't going to be beautiful in her red dress. She wasn't going to be beautiful in her dress at all. But one of her wishes would come true: Wearing this dress, she would certainly look different. No one would mistake her for Hallie now.

Father came out of the house carrying the milk pails. When he saw Mallie he ran to her.

"Why are you outside? What's wrong?" He saw the washtub and dress and stopped still. He put a hand under Mallie's chin and lifted it until she was looking at him. "What happened?"

Mallie tried to stop her tears. "The Gypsies—"

"Gypsies!" Father's face went dark with anger. "They broke into the house?"

"No." Mallie knew whom to blame. "I did it. I wanted to look different." She told Father about her visit to the camp.

Father knelt to look at the dress. "It's a proper mess," he said. "I don't know anything about dresses. Maybe your mother can fix it."

He looked up at Mallie. "She'll be upset, Mallie, with good reason. She worked hard so that you girls could look nice today." Mallie hung her head. Father nodded toward the house. "Go tell her," he said. "She's getting breakfast."

Mallie went. The walk to the house seemed very long.

Mother was kneading biscuit dough. Flour covered her hands so that it looked like she was wearing a pair of white gloves. She slapped the dough against the wooden counter and leaned her weight against it. Mallie watched from the doorway. A sudden coldness came over her. She swallowed, and swallowed again. She couldn't speak.

"Mallie!" Mother turned with a jump. "Good heavens, what's wrong? Are you sick?" She rushed to Mallie and put her arms around her. Mallie held herself stiff. She couldn't believe what she'd done.

"Tell me," Mother said, smoothing back Mallie's hair with a floury finger. "Tell me what's wrong."

"I'm sorry," Mallie whispered. She took Mother's hand and led her outside to the washtub.

Mother looked at the dress. Her face went

smooth. Mallie knew she was very angry indeed.

"Did you do this on purpose?" she asked Mallie.

Mallie burst into tears again. "It wasn't supposed to turn brown!"

"Can you fix it?" Father asked, coming out of the barn.

"Not by noontime," Mother said. "Mallie, what did you use?"

"Madder," Mallie said, remembering the word. "From the Gypsies."

Mother shook her head. "Take the tub up to the house," she said. "Then get ready for breakfast."

At that moment Hallie ran out the front door. She skipped toward them, her braids flying. "It's picnic day!" she called out. "Picnic day!"

She stopped short at the sight of Mallie's tears and looked at her in confusion. Mallie quit crying and squared her shoulders. She pointed to the tub. Hallie looked. Her mouth fell open. Bright pink splotches appeared on her cheeks. "You're ruining everything!" she shouted.

Hallie ran back to the house before Mallie could speak. She slammed the door so hard that the front windows rattled.

Mother and Father didn't move. Mallie looked at the ground. She waited for them to say something else. When they didn't, she grabbed one side of the tub and started to drag it toward the house. She stubbed her toe on a rock. The tub banged the back of her ankle. She bit her lip. She'd cried enough for one day.

Father took the tub out of Mallie's hands. He carried it to the porch and gently set it down. But when he passed Mallie on his way back to the barn, he didn't look at her at all.

13

Hallie's Dress

At breakfast everyone was angry. Mother asked Mallie to explain. Mallie described the Gypsy woman's powder. "It was supposed to be red," she said.

Mother sighed. "Madder comes from a plant," she said. "They used it back in my grandmother's day. Plant dyes aren't simple, Mallie. That's why we have synthetic dyes now. Did you use well water?"

Mallie nodded.

"It has iron in it," Mother said. "The iron turns fabric brown. You have to use rainwater for dyeing."

"I didn't know," Mallie said.

"I realize that," Mother said. "And did the

Gypsy tell you to throw the powder into cold water?"

Mallie shook her head. "She just said it would make my dress red."

"Why red?" asked Mother.

Hallie gave her a bitter look. "She wanted to look like a dirty Gypsy."

"They're not dirty," Mallie said.

"Girls!" Father put his hand flat on the table. He spoke to Mallie first. "Leave the Gypsies alone. Forever. If I hear that you've gone down to that camp again, I'll tan your backside. Understand?"

Mallie gulped and nodded. Father never hit them.

He turned to Hallie. "You leave your sister alone. She'll get her punishment from your mother and me, not from you."

"I don't want to go to the picnic with her," Hallie complained. Father looked at her. "Sorry," Hallie said hastily. "I'll go."

"You had both better shape up," Father said.

"You'll have to wear your school dress today," Mother told Mallie. "You'll be hot, but it's the only other decent dress you have."

"I can't," Mallie said. She looked at her plate. "I gave it to the Gypsies. For the madder."

The kitchen was so silent Mallie heard her own heart beating. Even Sarah seemed thunderstruck.

"Oh, Mallie," Mother said at last. "What will we do with you? I suppose you'll have to stay home."

"She can't," Hallie squeaked. "She's got half my poem."

Father's voice boomed like a hammer hitting metal. "She's going," he said. "It doesn't matter what she wears."

Mother had Mallie try on her old summer dress. Mallie squeezed her shoulders into it and yanked it over her head, but she couldn't button it. Mother pulled hard on the sides of the bodice and got the first button closed. It snapped off and shot across the kitchen, bouncing against Hallie's plate. Only Sarah laughed.

"You can wear Hallie's school dress," Mother decided. "No one will know it isn't yours."

They went upstairs to change. "Don't be angry at me," Mallie told Hallie. "You're going to look fine."

Hallie bared her teeth at Mallie. "I'm going to smile like this all day," she said, "so everyone can tell us apart. I'm not even going to speak to you."

14

The Wrecked *Hesperus*

Hallie kept her word. She was silent the whole way to the picnic, and once there she jumped down from the wagon and ran off. Mallie climbed down slowly.

"Take Sarah," Mother said.

Mallie reached up to lift Sarah down. "No!" Sarah said, smacking Mallie's hands.

"Stop it!" Mallie said.

"Mallie! Be nice."

"I'm trying!"

Hallie had found Ruthie. By the time Mallie carried Sarah over to them, Hallie had told Ruthie all about the dyed dress. Ruthie looked at Mallie with admiration and horror. "Is it really brown?" she asked.

Mallie set Sarah down. "No," she said. "It's

about half brown. If it was all brown, it would look better than it does."

"Weren't you scared to talk to the Gypsies?" Ruthie asked.

Mallie tossed her braids. "That Gypsy girl was nicer than Hallie."

Hallie rolled her eyes. Ruthie shook her head. "The mail-order bride is here," she said. "I saw her."

"What does she look like?" Mallie asked.

"Tall and mean," said Ruthie. "She looks like she never learned how to smile."

Mother called them to eat. When Mallie bent over to get a plate from the picnic basket, she heard a rip and felt something give in the back of Hallie's dress.

"What happened?" she asked, showing Hallie.

Hallie yelped. "Now you've ruined *my* dress!"

"All I did was bend over!"

Mother examined the dress. "The fabric's torn halfway around," she said. "I can't fix it now." She used her hatpin to hold the dress together.

"I can't recite a poem with a hatpin on my back," Mallie said. "I look ridiculous."

"Mallie." Mother sounded stern. "This is your doing, not mine and not Hallie's."

"You certainly look different now," Hallie said.

Mallie was too upset to eat. By the time Miss Lane gathered all the students together, she felt ready to be sick.

Hallie smoothed her sailor collar. For once Mallie wished she were dressed exactly like Hallie. She listened to the smallest first-grader stumble through "Twinkle, Twinkle, Little Star" and longed to be home in bed.

"Hallie and Matilda Graber." Miss Lane caught Mallie's eye and smiled. Mallie tried to smile back, but she couldn't. Her lips trembled. She followed Hallie to the front of the assembly. Her stomach lurched like a freshly caught catfish. She tried to stand so that the hatpin wouldn't show.

"Face front," Miss Lane murmured. Mallie turned her head but not her body. She heard a ripple of laughter from somewhere in the crowd. She felt her knees shake.

" 'The Wreck of the *Hesperus,*' by Henry Wadsworth Longfellow," said Hallie.

Mallie looked at the crowd. All of Cedarville was there. Everyone she knew, except the Gypsies. Even Mrs. Jenkins, somewhere. They probably all wondered why Mallie looked so ragged compared to Hallie. They probably knew; Hallie had probably told them.

With a shock, Mallie realized that Hallie had finished the first stanza. It was her turn. She opened her mouth. It was as though she'd opened a door in her head and let the words of the poem fly right out. She couldn't remember how to begin. She couldn't remember her first word, or her second. She couldn't remember any of it.

Hallie nudged her. Mallie panicked. She couldn't remember anything. Her mouth opened and shut like a dying fish's.

" 'Blue were her eyes as the fairy-flax,' " Ruthie prompted in a whisper. Ruthie had heard them practice.

"Blue were her eyes as the flairy-fax," Mallie said. *Flairy-fax! Oh, how awful!* she thought in dismay. Her face flamed.

" 'Her cheeks like the dawn of day.' " Miss Lane stood beside her. She quietly finished Mallie's part. Hallie stumbled through her next lines, and, after a short but terrifying pause, Miss Lane said the next. Mallie stood trembling and red while Hallie and Miss Lane finished the poem together. She wished the earth would open up and swallow her. She'd never felt so ashamed.

"I won't forgive you," Hallie said when they were back at the wagon. Mallie threw herself onto a pile of old feed sacks and cried. Mother put her arms around Mallie, but Hallie turned her back. "You did that on purpose," Hallie said. "I'll never speak to you again."

15

A Piano Lesson

The next few days were agony. Hallie did not speak to Mallie. She didn't even look at her. When Mallie spoke to Hallie, Hallie plugged her ears and hummed. Mother and Father were not angry about the poem, but they were still very angry about the Gypsy dye. They told Mallie she could not leave the yard. Mallie knew it was only the start of her punishment.

She spent most of her time playing outside with Sarah. She watched the road in case the Gypsies went by. She wanted to ask them how the dye was supposed to work. Meanwhile Mother bleached the dress and hung it outdoors in the sun. It lightened, but not enough.

"What if it doesn't go back to white?" Mallie

asked on Monday morning. Mother turned the dress over in her hand.

"I don't know," Mother said. She hung it back on the clothesline. "I won't make you another dress. We can't afford it, and if we could, I still wouldn't do it. Probably we'll have to overdye this one some other color."

"Oh." Nothing that would cover brown would be pretty.

"Why red?" Mother asked. "Of all colors, what made you want red?"

Mallie twisted her hands together. "The Gypsy girl looked so beautiful," she said. "So different." Mallie took a big breath. "She looked the way I feel, the way I want to be."

"Mallie!" Mother sounded truly shocked. "How can you say that? The Gypsies are nothing but wanderers. You have a house and a family."

Mallie didn't know what to say. She didn't want to actually *be* a Gypsy. She didn't want to leave her family. She just wanted to be the person she felt like instead of the person she looked like. Part of her was sorry that the dress was brown, but part of her—the Gypsy part—was glad. No matter what, when she wore it she would look different from Hallie.

That afternoon, while Sarah slept, Mother sat Hallie and Mallie down at the piano.

"Here is where we begin," she said. She played one of the white keys on the piano. "This is middle C. Here, Mallie, try it."

Mallie put her index finger on middle C. The note sounded, then gradually faded away.

"Pick your finger back up when you're through," Mother said. "Pretend your fingers are little hammers."

Hallie took a turn. She hit middle C sharp and quick, like a nail on the head.

"Not that hard!" said Mother.

"But you said hammer," Hallie answered.

"I don't mean it that way," said Mother. "Watch." She rippled off a trill of notes. Mallie's fingers could never move so fast.

Next Mother opened her book of exercises, the one that looked like marching ants. She pointed to the ladderlike lines. "These are the staffs. The top lines are the treble clef and the bottom lines are the bass clef."

Mallie nodded, even though she had no idea

what Mother meant. Hallie frowned and swung her feet.

Mother tried to explain. "The notes are all part of either the treble or the bass clef."

Mallie looked hard at the music and tried to understand. She didn't. "Where do the black keys go?" she asked.

"Don't worry about that yet," Mother said. She looked from one twin to the other. "I'm confusing you, aren't I?" Hallie and Mallie nodded. "I'm sorry," Mother said. "Bear with me, and it will make sense soon. Would you like to play something?"

"Yes," said Mallie.

"I guess so," said Hallie.

Mother pointed to the first finger exercise.

"I'd rather play a song," said Hallie. "I want to play 'Turkey in the Straw.' "

Mother laughed. "I'm sorry, but I don't have any song music. I mostly played classical pieces, and everything I have right now is too advanced for you girls to begin on. As soon as we can, we'll get a beginner book for you. But for now you can learn these exercises. Watch." Mother played the notes. "Mallie, you try."

Mallie stared at her fingers. She tried to follow Mother's example, but she missed several notes. It sounded terrible. Mallie was surprised to discover that finger exercises played incorrectly could sound much worse than finger exercises played correctly. "I'm sorry," she said.

"You're doing fine," Mother said. "Just remember to follow the notes on the page."

The notes on the page made no sense at all. Mallie tried again, with worse results. Hallie snorted through her nose. Mallie stuck her tongue out at Hallie.

"Here," Mother said, laying her hands over Mallie's. "Let me show you." She pushed Mallie's fingers down in order, moving them across the keyboard. "Start here," she said, playing a note, "and when you get to this note, you turn around and go back down."

Mallie nodded. She could do that. It was boring and it didn't sound like music, but she could do it.

"Your turn, Hallie," Mother said.

Hallie didn't move. "Can't we play real music?"

Mother smiled. "Soon, I promise. For now, just practice this exercise for half an hour a day. You'll be playing smoothly in no time."

Half an hour a day! Across Mother's back, Hallie and Mallie exchanged horrified looks. What a stupid way to spend the summer. Mallie remembered the Gypsy violin she'd heard on the last day of school. She remembered how it had made her dance right in the middle of the road. *That* was how music should be.

16

Mrs. Ellis to the Rescue

On Wednesday they had knitting circle. "Do I get to go?" Mallie asked. If so, it would be the first time since the picnic she'd been allowed off the farm.

"Knitting for the soldiers is our duty," Mother said.

Mallie was glad to have a duty. She walked upstairs to get Hallie. "Knitting circle time," she announced. Hallie looked up from the book she was reading. She closed it without a word and took her knitting bag out of a dresser drawer. "Could you hand me mine?" Mallie asked.

Hallie sighed. She picked up Mallie's knitting bag with two fingers and held it out at arm's length. Mallie took it. She hoped Hallie would forgive her soon.

When they passed the Gypsy camp, Mallie stood on tiptoe to see who was there. "Stop that, Mallie," Mother scolded.

"I thought I could ask them about my dress," Mallie said.

"They'll never tell you anything useful," Mother answered. "Stay away from them."

"Dirty thieves," Hallie added under her breath.

"They're not!" Mallie cried.

"They stole your school dress," Hallie said.

"It was old and it didn't fit me and I gave it to them," Mallie retorted. "They didn't steal it."

Mother looked grave. "They stole your trust," she said. "The Gypsies live by different rules than we do. You're making them out to be better than they are."

"Hallie's making them out to be worse than they are," Mallie said.

"Maybe. But two of our chickens disappeared last night, even though the door on the henhouse was latched."

"See?" Hallie said.

Mallie shook her head. There could have been a loose board in the henhouse. A weasel could have dug a hole to get in. Any number of things could have happened.

As they passed the Hawk farm, Mrs. Hawk and Ruthie and Bert fell in with them. The girls walked ahead while Mother and Mrs. Hawk exchanged news.

"Is your dress fixed yet?" Ruthie asked Mallie. Mallie shook her head. "Is Hallie talking to you?" Ruthie asked. Mallie shook her head. "Are you talking to me?" Ruthie continued.

Mallie smiled. "Yes."

Ruthie grinned. "Well, that's good. We missed you at church." Mallie had stayed home because she had nothing to wear. "And don't feel bad," Ruthie continued cheerfully. "I don't think anyone will laugh at you today. At least, not much."

Mallie hadn't even thought of that. "I should have stayed home," she said.

Hallie kicked a clod of dirt. "Are you going to talk to her all day?" she asked Ruthie.

Ruthie narrowed her eyes. "I'll talk to both of you as much as I want," she said. "This isn't my fight."

"It's not my fight, either," Hallie said, shooting a glance at Mallie. "Mallie's fighting, and she doesn't even know why."

"Yes, I do!" Mallie said. "I'm sick of being And Mallie. If you're not fighting, why aren't you talking to me?"

Hallie shrugged. She turned to Ruthie. "I don't like her much anymore," she said.

Mallie bit her lip. Sometimes she thought her heart might break.

The meeting was at Mrs. Hendricks's house. She greeted them politely without fuss, let Mother and Mrs. Hawk put the baby carriages in the kitchen, and led them all into the crowded parlor.

"Well," Maude said cheerfully from the far end of the room, "if it isn't Miss Flairy-Fax! Hello, Mallie!"

Mallie felt her face go red. Her feet seemed stuck in the carpet.

Mrs. Ellis stood up. She walked forward and put her arms around Mallie. "My dear," she said, "don't you listen to a word. The same thing happened to me at my school picnic, years and years ago. I opened my mouth and could not speak. You knew that poem by heart, didn't you?" She patted Mallie's shoulder.

Mallie leaned against her. "I did," she said. "I knew the whole thing."

"She really did," Ruthie added.

"See?" Mrs. Ellis said. "We won't say anything more about it." She led Mallie to the davenport and patted the seat. Mallie scooted to the floor. Mrs. Ellis sat. "Poor thing," she continued. "I knew something was wrong the moment I saw you. That was the only time in my life I've seen you dressed differently than your twin. I thought, *Good gracious, what has happened? The Graber twins don't look the same.*"

Mother cleared her throat. "I'm afraid we had a small accident at home. I couldn't get Mallie's dress finished in time."

Mrs. Ellis continued to pat Mallie's shoulder. "These things happen," she said. "Never mind, Hallie, never mind."

"I'm Mallie," Mallie said meekly.

"Of course you are, dear. I never can tell."

Mrs. Hendricks opened the meeting. "Notable by her absence is our new neighbor, Mrs. Jenkins," she said. "I have called on her once again. She still refuses to join us."

The mail-order bride! Mallie had forgotten about her.

"I'll call on her tomorrow," Mallie's mother said. "I've been meaning to do so."

On the way home Mallie dragged her feet through the dirt. At last she spoke. "Why do Hallie and I always have to dress alike?"

"To be fair," Mother said gently. "I wouldn't ever want one of you to think I favored the other. How would you feel if Hallie had a fancier dress?"

Mallie wouldn't care if Hallie's dress was fancy. "I always thought you did it because it was easier to make two dresses the same," she said.

"It is," Mother admitted, "but that's not why I do it. You're the same age, and you deserve to be treated the same."

"Oh," Hallie cut in. "Then why is Sarah's new dress the same too?"

Mother gave Hallie a sharp look. She didn't respond.

That night Mallie lay in bed beside Hallie. The air was so cool that they'd pulled their coverlet up to their shoulders and let the cats sleep on the bed again. Light from the full moon shone through the open window and made the coverlet glow.

"I wish you'd talk to me," Mallie said.

"Why?" said Hallie.

"You complained to Mother about our dresses."

"I didn't complain," said Hallie.

"What you said was the same as complaining."

"So?"

"So you wouldn't have said it if you didn't feel the same way about the dresses I do," said Mallie. "It's silly for you to be mad at me. Plus, you were really horrible at the picnic." She spoke more loudly. "It wasn't my fault your dress ripped. I never would have forgotten my part of the poem on purpose. It was the most embarrassing moment of my life. You should have been nice to me. Ruthie was, and she's not even my sister."

"It was the most embarrassing moment of my life, too."

"Nobody laughed at *you*."

Hallie sighed. She rolled over.

"Turn back around," Mallie said.

"No," said Hallie.

"You know I'm right," Mallie said. "You just won't admit it."

Hallie didn't move.

"Admit it," Mallie said. She knew she was right.

Hallie still didn't move.

"Admit it," Mallie said again.

"No," Hallie said. But after a moment her hand crept across the top of the coverlet and encircled Mallie's wrist. "I guess I'll talk to you," she said.

17

Mrs. Jenkins

The next morning after breakfast Mother put on her hat and gloves. She pulled Sarah's shoes onto her feet. Sarah kicked in protest.

"You girls can take care of yourselves for an hour," Mother said. "It would be a good time to practice the piano."

"Are you going to see Mrs. Jenkins?" Mallie asked.

"Can we come?" said Hallie.

"Yes and no," Mother said firmly. "You may come some other time."

They hung about the porch and watched her go. "Let's follow," Mallie suggested.

Hallie grinned. "Let's get Ruthie first."

They ran through the fields to the Hawk farm. When they got there, they found that Ruthie was just about to go get them. "My mother's gone with your mother," she reported. "If we run the back way, we can beat them there."

In a few minutes Hallie, Mallie, and Ruthie were on Mr. Jenkins's land. The house sat quietly, without a soul in sight. A cloud of dust in a far-off field showed where Mr. Jenkins was plowing for winter wheat.

"Maybe she's not home," Mallie whispered.

"Let's climb the cherry trees," Ruthie whispered back. "We can spy from there."

It was a daring idea. Mr. Jenkins's cherry orchard bordered his house on its long side. The trees were in fruit; the leaves didn't completely cover the cherry-laden branches. It was not a good place to hide.

Still, Mallie couldn't see a better one. Mr. Jenkins didn't have shrubs or flower beds. "If we're quiet, they might not notice us," she said. They pulled themselves into the trees.

Mallie made herself comfortable on a thick branch. She couldn't see into the windows of the house, but she could see the door, and she would be able to hear if Mother talked loudly. She looked over at Hallie and Ruthie. The trees hid them better than she would have guessed.

"Don't move," Hallie whispered. "They're coming."

Mallie heard the scrunch of the baby carriages as Mother and Mrs. Hawk wheeled up the drive. She saw Mrs. Hawk rap firmly on the door.

"Good morning," Mrs. Hawk said.

Mallie strained to get a clear view. Mrs. Jenkins was tall, as Ruthie had said. She was neither fat nor thin, well corseted, and very upright. She was not young, but she wasn't as old as Mother. She did not smile at her visitors. Mallie tried to imagine her smiling and could not.

Mrs. Hawk introduced herself and Mrs. Graber. She handed Mrs. Jenkins a loaf of freshly baked bread. "We're your closest neighbors," she told Mrs. Jenkins. "We've come to welcome you to Cedarville."

"Thank goodness," Mrs. Jenkins said. "I thought you'd come to talk me into joining the Red Cross. I've been expecting an indignant delegation."

Mrs. Hawk looked taken aback. Mallie smothered a laugh with the back of her hand. A branch on Hallie's tree began to shake.

"I'd invite you in for tea," Mrs. Jenkins continued, "only I haven't got any. Mr. Jenkins prefers coffee. I'm going to town for supplies soon, but not until I get the house fixed up. It's still a mess. I admire it, but Mr. Jenkins did not do much in the way of cleaning. Good day to you both."

Mallie had never heard a person speak quite so forthrightly. She began to like Mrs. Jenkins, frown and all.

Mother stepped forward with a swish of skirts. "But we *have* come to discuss the Red Cross," she said. "Whether you support it or not, or support the war or not, you should join. Cedarville is a small town. It is a patriotic one."

Mrs. Jenkins met Mother's eyes. "You mean that all the ladies will fuss about me, and talk, and avoid me forever, unless I plant a war garden and knit a hundred stockings."

"Unfortunately—" Mother began.

"The Red Cross does important work," Mrs. Hawk cut in. "Think of our brave boys in France."

"One of those brave boys in France was my first husband," Mrs. Jenkins said sharply. "Whether he died wearing the stockings I knit for him, I couldn't say."

Mrs. Hawk looked shocked. Mother looked sympathetic. To Mallie's surprise, she put her hand on Mrs. Jenkins's shoulder. Mrs. Jenkins let her.

"Grief is a terrible burden," Mother said, so quietly that Mallie had to strain to hear. "It is easier when it's shared. You will find that many of us do understand. Whether or not you join the Red Cross, I hope you'll come to my house for tea." She turned and began to push Sarah back up the driveway. Mrs. Jenkins said nothing. After a moment Mrs. Hawk followed Mother.

Mallie felt shaken. How had Mother known exactly the right thing to say?

For a moment Mrs. Jenkins stood as in a trance. Then she shook her head briskly. "You kids get out of those trees and skedaddle," she shouted. "I've got work enough to do."

18

In the Cherry Orchard

"One-two-three-four-five-four-three-two-one," Mallie chanted as she played the piano exercise. Mother had said to play steadily. Counting helped.

It was the next morning. At breakfast Hallie had nearly spilled the beans about Mrs. Jenkins. "Do you think she'll come to tea?" she had asked.

"Who?" Mother said.

"Mrs. Jenkins," Hallie said. She added quickly, "Since you called on her, doesn't she have to call on you?"

"No one has to do anything," Mother said. Then she smiled. "She didn't invite us in yesterday, but guess what I saw through the door! Mrs. Jenkins has a fine piano."

"One-two-three-four-five-four-three-two-one." Mallie wondered if Mrs. Jenkins played *real* music on her piano. Mother pounded her way through the exercise books with frightening efficiency but still hadn't played anything close to a song.

Hallie poked her head into the parlor. "Aren't you done?"

"Not until the clock strikes," Mallie said. "I started at ten-thirty exactly, so I can't quit until eleven." She reached the end of the exercise, let her hands rest for a moment, and began again.

Hallie sat down on the end of the bench. She played a few low notes. "I'm not doing this for a full half hour."

"It's not that bad," Mallie said. "Maybe if we learn the exercises really well, Mother will let us play real music."

Hallie sniffed. "When? She's got three whole books of exercises." She tossed her head. "I can't stand this piano. I wish Father'd traded for an icebox instead."

The clock struck the hour. Mallie scooted over on the bench. "Your turn."

Hallie shook her head. "Let's go spy on Mrs. Jenkins instead."

Mrs. Jenkins was standing in her orchard. She waved them over as they came through the fields. "You're the kids from the trees," she said.

"Yes, ma'am," Mallie said.

"Let me guess." Mrs. Jenkins looked from her to Hallie. "You're sisters."

Mallie felt herself flush. "Yes, ma'am," she repeated.

"Well, where's the third one?"

"Ruthie lives over there," Hallie said, pointing. "Our farm is that way."

"Have you grown up on a farm?" Mrs. Jenkins asked.

"Mostly," said Mallie.

"Then tell me, what do I do with these cherry trees?"

Mallie looked at Hallie. What did she mean?

"Do I shake them, like apple trees?" Mrs. Jenkins asked. "Or do the cherries fall off on their own when they're ripe?"

"Oh, no," Mallie said. "You've got to climb up the trees and pick them."

"One cherry at a time?" asked Mrs. Jenkins.

"Well," said Hallie, "you can grab handfuls."

Mrs. Jenkins plucked a cherry off a nearby branch. She ate it and spat the stone into her hand. "I was afraid of that," she said. "I come from Boston, a city on the ocean. Do you know that?"

Hallie nodded. "Mrs. Ellis says she hopes you're not stuck up like most New Englanders."

Mrs. Jenkins sighed. "I may live to regret all of my life, instead of just the first twenty-five years," she said. "So, after I climb up all the trees and pick all the cherries, then what do I do? With the cherries, I mean."

"Pie is good," said Mallie.

"Or preserves," said Hallie.

"Mother makes a cobbler sometimes," Mallie added.

Mrs. Jenkins sighed. "And how do I remove the pits?"

Mallie frowned. "With a knife," she said.

"I'm not actually stupid," Mrs. Jenkins said with a glimmer of a smile. "I can handle oysters, mussels, and crabs better, I daresay, than any other woman in this town. But cherries are new to me. They sound like more work than they're worth." She dropped the cherry pit from her hand. "Run along home, girls. I'm not yet ready for entertaining. Tell your mother to expect me for tea on Saturday. Tell her I will join the Red Cross."

19

Bass Farm

That afternoon Mother listened to them play. Mallie plowed through her exercise without too many mistakes. Hallie stumbled and was awful. "Look at the page," Mother said, pointing to the music. "Both of you keep looking at your hands."

Mallie didn't know how to say that the music on the page still didn't make sense.

"We don't like this," Hallie said. "It's not a song. It isn't pretty."

Mother nodded. "I know," she said. "Music is more fun when it's pretty. Let's try something else." She picked up her hymnal, opened it, and set it on the music rack. "Here. Your father will like this one. It's his favorite."

Hallie groaned aloud. "It's too hard."

"No, you can do it. Listen." Mother played the hymn, slowly but with feeling. It was easy for her. "Try it," she told Mallie. "It starts here." She pointed to a note on the keyboard.

Mallie frowned in concentration. She placed her hands where Mother directed and stared at the music. She tried to remember which notes Mother had played. To her surprise, her first few notes sounded correct.

"Good, good," Mother said. "Keep going." But after a moment Mallie became hopelessly confused. She stopped playing.

"I'm sorry," she said.

"Don't be sorry," Mother said. "We'll figure it out." From the bedroom where she'd been napping, Sarah began to cry. Mother got up. "Go back to the exercise today. We'll try the hymn again tomorrow."

"Phew!" Hallie whispered when Mother was gone. "That was awful!"

Mallie nodded, but she felt disappointed. She tried to play the first line of the hymn again.

" 'Oh, Lord my God,' " Hallie warbled off-key, " 'when I in awesome wonder—' " She broke off. "You're not awesomely wonderful, Mallie; you're wonderfully awful. And I'm worse. We're terrible."

Each note on the page is a note on the keyboard, Mallie told herself. *I should be able to figure it out.*

Hallie picked up a pen Mother had left lying on a side table. "Maybe we should add some more notes to the music," she said mischievously. "Maybe then it would sound better."

"In the *hymnal*?" Mallie was aghast.

Hallie grinned. "Maybe then Mother would leave us alone."

Hallie had to be joking. Before Mallie could reply, the front door flew open. Ruthie ran into the room.

"We're going to Bass Farm!" she shouted. She was sweaty and panting. She collapsed on the rug. "Bass Farm! Tomorrow! Father just told us. He's taking us all in the wagon."

"Oh, lucky you!" Mallie said. She knew all about Bass Farm. It was in Fort Wayne. It had beautiful gardens, a deer park, and even buffalo. "We've never been."

"You're invited, too!" Ruthie said. "And we're

going to take a picnic. We're going to be gone the whole day."

"Yippee!" Hallie shouted.

"Will they let us pet the buffalo?" Mallie asked.

"I don't know," Ruthie said. "Maude said she rode one when she went. I think she was lying."

They thought for a moment. "She mostly lies," said Hallie.

"We might get to ride one," said Mallie. It was barely imaginable. She had never even seen a buffalo. "Do they have saddles?"

"They must," Ruthie said. She grabbed Mallie's hand on one side and Hallie's on the other. "Let's go tell your mother."

Sarah was crying and beating Mother with her fists. "Too hot!" she wailed. Sarah always woke up crabby.

"We're going to Bass Farm with Ruthie tomorrow!" Hallie burst out.

"With all the Hawks!" Mallie added. "We're going to see the buffalo!"

Mother raised her eyebrows.

"If we may," Hallie added quickly. "May we

please go to Bass Farm with Ruthie and her family tomorrow?"

Mother smiled, but she didn't look happy. "You may," she said. "Mallie will have to stay home."

"But Mother!" Hallie protested. "Why? We're going to ride the buffalo!"

"Please, Mrs. Graber!" Ruthie said. "It won't be any fun without Mallie."

Mallie didn't say a word. She knew why Mother had said no. She knew nothing on earth would change Mother's mind.

"Ruthie, I'm sure you and Hallie will have a nice time," Mother said. "Tomorrow Mallie is going to redye her new dress."

20

A Bitter Heart

"Just because I deserve to be punished doesn't mean you *have* to punish me," Mallie said.

"Yes, it does," Mother replied. Mallie could see she had been biding her time.

"You spoiled everything," Hallie said when they went to bed that night. "You wanted to look like a Gypsy."

"I wouldn't mind being a Gypsy," Mallie said. "I bet they get to go to Bass Farm."

"You're nutty," Hallie said.

"You don't have to go," Mallie said. "You could stay home and help me."

Hallie gave Mallie a troubled look. "Oh, go," Mallie said. "I don't care. At least one of us will get to see the buffalo."

"I'll stay home if you want me to," Hallie said. "It won't be as much fun without you."

For the first time all day, Mallie felt tears come to her eyes. "Go," she said. "You can tell me about it."

"Maybe they have photographs of the buffalo," Hallie said. She pulled the coverlet down on the bed. "You ought to pour ink on that hymnbook."

Mallie had forgotten about it. Anger bubbled up in her chest. "Maybe I will," she said.

In the morning she woke with a heart full of bitterness. Hallie skipped off to the Hawk farm carrying a box of cookies. Mallie stabbed the yolk of her breakfast egg. She watched it run in yellow streams across her plate. "I'm not hungry," she said.

Mother took her plate away. "Put on your stockings and shoes," she said. "We'll go into town to buy the dye."

On the way she kicked rocks until Mother told her to stop. "Quit sulking," Mother said. "You knew you would be punished. If you didn't like your dress, you should have said so."

"I didn't get the chance," Mallie said. "You

bought the fabric and cut it out before Hallie and I knew."

Mother looked angry. "Don't talk back," she said.

A few minutes later, they passed the Gypsy camp. Mallie slowed her steps. She couldn't hear any music, but she could smell eggs frying.

Mother looked at her. "The Gypsies will be moving on soon," she said. "Folks in town are starting to lose patience with them."

Mallie kicked another rock. Everyone blamed the Gypsies for everything. Mallie couldn't believe the world was so unfair.

At McClennan's store Mother lingered over the display of dyes. "I suppose dark brown would be best," she said. "It would cover the stains. But I've never thought you looked good in brown."

"Perhaps black?" Mrs. McClennan suggested. She walked over to help, carrying her baby on her hip. She ran the store now because Mr. McClennan was in the army. Mallie glared at her.

Mother raised her eyebrows. "In black she'd look like she was in mourning. Mallie, what color do you like?"

"Red," Mallie said.

Mother gave her a stern look. She picked up a packet of dark blue dye and one of burgundy and considered them both. Mallie wandered over to the window and looked out.

She gasped in delight. "The Gypsies are coming!"

Mrs. McClennan gasped in horror. She hurried to the door and tried to close it just as several small Gypsy children ran in. The girl Mallie's age followed them. "Get out!" yelled Mrs. McClennan. Her baby began to wail.

The Gypsy children scattered in all directions, giggling. A fat Gypsy woman came in. She shook her fist in Mrs. McClennan's face and shouted. Mrs. McClennan shouted back. They began to argue. The baby screamed. Sarah cried.

The Gypsy girl came up to Mallie and smiled.

Mallie didn't smile back. She was too upset by Mrs. McClennan's behavior. Why couldn't the Gypsies come into the store? It wasn't fair!

"Good morning again," the girl said to Mallie. She took a packet of brass buttons off the countertop in front of Mallie and put them into the pocket of her skirt. Then she took some needles and several bright skeins of embroidery thread.

Mallie was astonished. The Gypsies were stealing! She had truly never believed it before.

The girl walked past the counter in front of Mallie. She helped herself to more and more items from the store. *The pocket in her skirt must be huge,* Mallie thought.

One of the younger children ran up to the girl with a handful of candy. The girl laughed. She took the child by the hand, opened the window at the front of the store, and lifted the child out to the porch. One by one the other children ran to her, and she lifted them out. Finally the girl herself started to climb out the window.

Mallie ran up to her and grabbed her arm. "You shouldn't be doing this," she said. "It's wrong!"

The girl gently removed Mallie's hand. For a moment they looked at each other. Then the girl winked at Mallie and swung herself out the window. She whistled shrilly and ran down the road after the smaller children, who were already far away.

At the sound of the whistle, the Gypsy

woman quit arguing. Mrs. McClennan moved to block the door, but the woman slipped out and ran away.

It had been planned, Mallie realized. The woman had meant to argue all along, to distract Mrs. McClennan while the children filled their pockets.

Mallie walked back to her mother's side. "They were stealing," she said. "They were stealing everything."

21

Blue Dye, Black Ink

Mother nodded. "I saw," she said. She soothed Sarah against her shoulder and handed Mallie a packet of dye. "I've thought of a clever way to save your dress. We'll dye it deep navy blue. I'll buy some white ribbon to trim the collar, and some navy ribbon to trim the collar of Hallie's dress. See? It will look like we planned it all along."

Mallie began to tremble. "You don't understand!" she said. "The whole point of dyeing the dress was so that I wouldn't look like Hallie! I'd rather keep my dress speckled brown!"

Mother's mouth tightened. "For that remark, I should let you." She asked Mrs. McClennan to measure out the ribbon.

Mallie fumed. She would look like Hallie's

shadow! It would be worse than just looking like Hallie. "Can't we do something else?" she asked Mother.

"No," Mother said. "I have had enough from you. Behave." She paid for the ribbon and dye and hauled Mallie and Sarah outside. "You're acting like a baby, Mallie. Glory, but I felt ashamed in there!"

"Matilda," Mallie said.

Mother plunked Sarah back into the carriage. "You'd do better not to speak to me just now." She pushed the carriage down the road.

Mallie followed, tears of rage in her eyes. It was not fair, not fair! Hallie was riding a buffalo, the Gypsies were thieves, and her dress was going to look worse than ugly.

By the time they reached home Mallie's anger had hit a fever pitch. Under Mother's direction, she boiled her dress in navy dye. She rinsed it and hung it on the clothesline. Then she went into the parlor and looked at the bottle of ink and the pen. She sat down on the piano bench and removed the hymnal from the rack. She uncapped the bottle of ink, set it on the piano, and dipped the pen.

Mallie drew a black line through the notes on the top of the page. Then she stopped. Suddenly it seemed like such a silly thing to do. A wicked thing, to destroy a hymn.

A drop of ink fell from the pen, blotting the first words: *Oh, Lord my God*— Mallie touched it with her finger. The dark color looked like her newly dyed dress.

She set down the pen. All the anger seemed to flow out of her. She felt empty and lonely and sad. She propped the hymnal back on the rack. In a few minutes the ink would dry. The book was not much damaged after all. She picked up the bottle and started to screw the cap on.

"Mallie!" Mother's shout made her jump. The cap from the ink bottle flew out of her hand. A wave of black ink splashed against the piano. It covered the hymnal and dripped onto the keys.

Mallie jumped up so quickly that she knocked the bench over. "I didn't mean to!" She grabbed the lace doily from the top of the piano and swabbed at the wet ink.

Mother snatched the doily from her hands. "Out!" She pointed at the door. "Out! Now! Go!"

Mallie ran through the kitchen and out the back door. She went around the house and looked through the parlor window. Mother was wiping the ink from the piano keys with her apron. She didn't look angry. She looked as though she might cry.

Mallie slunk to the ground, heartsick. She'd ruined everything this summer: her dress, her poem, now Mother's piano. She wished she could start over. She buried her head in her arms and cried. She was an awful person. She was no better than the Gypsies.

The Gypsies! Mallie wished she could see them just one more time. Maybe she could see them the way they really were. She quit crying and wiped her eyes. She thought of looking into the parlor again, but she couldn't stand to. Instead she got up and walked through the tall grass to the Gypsy camp.

The Gypsies were gone.

22

Losing the Piano

Mallie walked through the deserted camp. Coals smoldered in the ashes of the cook fire, so she knew the Gypsies hadn't been gone long. She wondered if they had made their plan to leave before they raided McClennan's store. Perhaps it had been a sort of good-bye.

She searched for a while among the bits of trash left behind. She found a pile of feathers that might have come from one of Mother's missing hens and a button from her old school dress. She didn't find any of the fabric from the dress itself. Mallie hoped the Gypsies had put it to good use and not just ripped it into rags. She hoped one of the little Gypsy children would wear it next winter and keep warm.

Down by the river crossing, the Gypsies' horses had churned the mud into ridges. Mallie picked her way into the slow-moving water. She stood ankle-deep and let her toes dig into the sandy bottom. She dreaded going home. How could she face Mother?

She walked downstream. When she climbed onto dry land again, she was on Mr. Jenkins's farm. She walked toward his house, slowly, aimlessly, with no real idea in her head except that she didn't want to go home.

The front door was propped open. On both sides of it, freshly dug garden beds were laid out with sticks and pieces of string. It was late in the year for planting, but evidently Mrs. Jenkins was going to try.

Mallie poked her head in the door. Mr. and Mrs. Jenkins were sitting in their parlor on a pair of straight-backed chairs. Mr. Jenkins had an empty plate on his lap. They didn't notice Mallie.

Mr. Jenkins looked up at Mrs. Jenkins shyly and smiled. "It's been a comfort having you here," he said.

Mrs. Jenkins looked at her hands. "I'm glad," she said. She raised her eyes at Mr. Jenkins and smiled.

"Hello," Mallie said.

Mrs. Jenkins turned without haste. "Hello, Mallie Graber," she said.

Mrs. Jenkins's piano took up the whole parlor wall. Mallie stared at it. Its keys were bright white.

"Can we help you?" asked Mrs. Jenkins.

Mr. Jenkins cleared his throat. "Is something wrong?"

A sob rose in Mallie's chest. "Everything," she said. She slipped away from them and ran for home.

When she reached Mother's herb garden her courage failed. She sank to the ground among the strong-smelling plants. What could she do to make things right? She would gladly be And Mallie for the rest of her life and dress identically to Hallie for as long as they both lived if it would save Mother's piano. She lay flat against the earth, her face to the sky. Out of the corner of her eye she could just see the navy sleeve of her dyed dress, flapping in the wind.

I'm so sorry, she thought. *I'll wear it, I promise. I'll be grateful. I'll be good.* The smell of basil and rosemary washed over her. She fell asleep.

Hallie shook her awake. Mallie sat up quickly and grabbed Hallie's arm.

"It's okay," Hallie said gently. "Mother saw you sleeping. She told me to come get you."

"Did she tell you what happened?"

"The piano's fine," Hallie said. "The ink wiped off the keys. It came off the wooden parts, too."

"What about the hymnal?"

"The first pages are ruined," Hallie said. "So is Mother's doily."

Mallie winced, though she knew she should be thankful. The piano was saved. "Mother will hate me," she said. "I started to write in the hymnal, but I could see how foolish it was—I was just so angry—and then . . . She's not going to believe me, Hallie. It's been the worst day."

Hallie squeezed Mallie's hand. "She doesn't hate you," she said. "She's not angry. She's mostly disappointed. I told her how we don't like to play." Hallie paused. "*Father*'s angry. He said we aren't to go near that piano ever again."

Mallie nodded.

"It's awful to disappoint Mother," Hallie said.

"Did you ride the buffalo?" Mallie asked.

Hallie wrinkled her nose. "Maude lies. Nobody gets to ride the buffalo. The man taking care of them said so. They were smashing good buffalo, though. One had a calf."

"I'm glad you're home," Mallie said.

"Mr. Hawk said maybe he'd take us again next year. Charlie got lost once, but nothing else bad happened. We ate watermelon." Hallie plucked a piece of lavender. "Are you going to talk to Mother?"

Mallie nodded.

"I'll come," Hallie said.

"Better not," said Mallie.

Hallie agreed. "I'll take Sarah for a walk," she said. "That way you can be alone."

Mallie smoothed her hair and dress. She walked toward the house. Suddenly she heard music coming from the parlor. It was real music—low, steady, throbbing music that seemed to flow out the open windows and glide across the grass. It sounded like wind blowing through a wheat field, like night air in the spring. It was beautiful. Mallie had never heard anything like it before.

She tiptoed through the back door. Mother sat at the piano, wholly absorbed. Mallie stood and listened. Mother played for a very long time. When she finished, Mallie wished there were more. She sagged against the door frame. This was what she had lost. She wasn't allowed to play the piano anymore.

23

Moonlight

"What was that?" Mallie whispered.

Mother turned slowly, as though she were still hearing the music in her head. "The 'Moonlight' Sonata, by Beethoven," she said. "It's supposed to sound like moonlight."

"It does," Mallie said. "That's exactly what it sounds like. It's beautiful."

"I'm glad you liked it," Mother said. Hallie was right. She didn't look angry.

Mallie walked forward. "I didn't mean to spill that ink," she said. "Truly I didn't. I did mean to write a little bit in the hymnal, and I know that was very wrong, but I never, ever meant to hurt the piano."

"I'm glad," Mother said quietly. "I was saddened to think you would have done such a thing."

"I'm sorry," Mallie said.

"Hallie told me that you don't like playing the piano. I wish you had said so right away."

"I do like it," Mallie said. "Hallie's wrong. I want to play."

Mother ran her finger over the keyboard. "Maybe in another year or two," she said. She got up and came over to Mallie's side. "I don't understand what has gotten into you this summer. You don't normally behave like this."

The Gypsies, Mallie thought forlornly. *The Gypsies got into me.*

"However." Mother blew out her breath. "You're ten years old."

Mallie frowned.

"When I was ten years old, nothing in my life made sense, either," Mother continued. "My big sister was mean, and my younger siblings were dreadful pests." She put her arm around Mallie.

"What did you do?" Mallie asked.

"I turned eleven," Mother said. She laughed. "I don't know why that year was so difficult for me, but it was. This summer is hard for you. Maybe next year will be Hallie's turn."

Mallie leaned into Mother's shoulder. "Can you please call me Matilda?" she asked.

"I can," Mother said. "I'd rather call you Mallie, though. I've always liked calling you Mallie. And you're wrong about being second. Your name, Mallie, came first."

"What do you mean?" asked Mallie.

"When you were born we named you Matilda, but we planned to call you Mallie. We named Hallie Hannah Alice, but calling you Mallie and Hannah sounded silly, and so did Hannah and Mallie. Eventually we started calling your sister Hallie, to match you."

"I didn't know that," Mallie said.

"I didn't realize it was important," Mother said. "May I still call you Mallie?"

"I guess so," Mallie said. "As long as you let me tell Hallie I was first."

24

Piano School

The next morning Mother played the "Moonlight" Sonata again. She followed it with another long piece that was almost as lovely. Mallie ached inside.

"What's wrong?" Hallie asked her. "You look swoony."

"I wish we could play that," Mallie said.

Hallie sniffed. "Good riddance," she said. She was sewing a stuffed buffalo out of fabric scraps for Sarah to play with. Mallie was sewing the ribbon trim onto her sailor dress. The navy dye had worked well.

Mallie looked at Hallie. An idea popped into her head. It was a good one, but she would need Hallie's cooperation. "Mother's *awfully* disappointed," she said.

"I know." Hallie bent over her work. Her mouth compressed the way Mother's sometimes did. "You don't need to tell me. I didn't do anything wrong, and she's still disappointed with me."

"You told her we didn't want to play the piano," Mallie said. "I think it's breaking her heart."

"She's not that upset," Hallie said.

"I think she is," Mallie said. "I think she'd feel better if we each learned to play a song. Just one song. Probably she'd feel a lot better then."

Hallie bit a stray thread. "We can't. We're not allowed to touch the piano."

"We could touch Mrs. Jenkins's piano," Mallie said.

Hallie stared. "Says who?" she asked. "You haven't talked to Mrs. Jenkins about it."

"No," Mallie admitted. "But I'm going to."

"She's scary," Hallie said. "She's not going to let us."

"She's not scary. I don't even think she's that mean. She would probably like it if we asked to play. And Mother would be so happy." Mallie kept her head down.

"Okay," Hallie said at last. "But *you* have to talk to Mrs. Jenkins."

"No," Mrs. Jenkins said. She held the door of her house half shut behind her. "I'm charmed by your interest, but I am not opening a piano school."

"Please," Mallie said.

"No."

Mallie had thought it might come to bargaining. "We'll pick all your cherries for you," she said.

"Mallie!" Hallie said.

Mrs. Jenkins smiled. She came out the door and pulled it shut behind her. "Let me be sure I understand," she said. "Both of you want to be able to play one whole song? That would take a lot of teaching. It would be worth more than a few cherries."

"You've got bushels of cherries," Hallie said.

"We'll help you pit and can them, too," Mallie said.

"Mallie!" squeaked Hallie.

Mrs. Jenkins laughed. It was the first time Mallie had heard her laugh. It was a pleasant sound. "That's a deal," she said. "When we're all through, I'll make more cherry pie. I made my first one yesterday, and Mr. Jenkins seemed to like it. Come into the house, girls. I'm your new piano teacher."

She let them into her parlor. She lifted the lid of the piano bench and pulled out some dusty music books. "What do you want to learn? If I don't have it, I can probably improvise."

"Turkey in the Straw," Hallie said.

"Done! Mallie?"

Mallie smiled. "The 'Moonlight' Sonata."

25

Victory

Mrs. Jenkins's smile disappeared. "Teaching you to play the 'Moonlight' Sonata would take me ten years," she said. "Have you ever heard it?"

"Mother plays it," Mallie said.

"Then you know how difficult it is. Pick something else."

Mallie looked at the floor. She tried not to cry.

"I know another piece by Beethoven you might be able to play," Mrs. Jenkins said. "It's soft and pretty, too. It's called 'Für Elise.' "

Mallie shrugged. "I don't care."

"I'll find the music for it." Mrs. Jenkins dropped the bench lid. "Your first lesson will start tomorrow at nine o'clock. After that we'll can cherries until noon. You can start picking them now. There are bushel baskets in the shed beside the barn."

"Glory!" Hallie said as they let themselves out of the house. "What a mess you've gotten us into! Hours of work when we could have played our piano at home for free!"

Mallie had forgotten that Mrs. Jenkins was coming to tea. By the time she and Hallie saw Mother mixing a pitcher of her special company lemonade, Mrs. Jenkins was already at the door. It was too late to warn her that the piano lessons were a secret.

"Mallie, don't squirm," Mother said as she sat down with Mrs. Jenkins in the parlor. "If you have an itch, take care of it in the kitchen."

Mrs. Jenkins nodded at the piano. "Do the girls play?" she asked.

"No!" Hallie said.

Mother frowned at Hallie. "I'm afraid they don't have an interest," she said. "Go into the kitchen, girls. You may have your snack there."

"Ah, well." Mrs. Jenkins sank back into her chair. "Perhaps they will develop an interest in time." She winked at Mallie.

Mallie dragged Hallie out of the room. "It's okay," she whispered.

They crept partway up the stairs, where they could listen without being seen. Mother and Mrs. Jenkins talked of weather and crops, and of the best stores for shopping in town. Mallie yawned.

"I've swallowed my pride and apologized to that old harpy Mrs. Hendricks," Mrs. Jenkins said abruptly. Mallie stifled a giggle. Mrs. Hendricks was Mother's friend. "I told her I thought there were two branches of the Red Cross in the area and I had intended to join the other one. We both apologized for our misunderstanding, I've signed up and paid my dollar, and now we'll have peace in this village, if not in the world."

"I think that's wise," Mother said.

"I think it's spineless," Mrs. Jenkins shot back. "However, I've burned my bridges and will probably live here the rest of my natural span. I don't wish to be the most disliked woman in town."

"Mrs. Hendricks has two sons in France," Mother said.

"Are they both alive?"

There was silence. Mallie imagined Mother nodding.

"Then she doesn't know how I feel," Mrs. Jenkins said. "I suppose you all think it's awful, my marrying a man while still grieving for another. Let me assure you, I have been perfectly honest with Mr. Jenkins."

There was another silence. This time Mallie couldn't imagine Mother doing anything.

Then Mother spoke in a low voice. "I lost three babies before Hallie and Mallie," she said. "The first died at birth. The other pregnancies didn't get that far."

Hallie and Mallie stared at each other. They remembered their brother, Samuel, who'd died a week after his birth only four years before. Three other babies? Mother and Father had never said a word. Silently Hallie squeezed Mallie's hand.

"Then you understand," Mrs. Jenkins said softly.

"Yes," Mother said.

Mallie pressed her ear against the wall.

"Yes," Mother said again, so quietly that Mallie had to close her eyes and concentrate to hear. "Hallie and Mallie are my victory."

26

The Lord Giveth

"Don't say anything," Hallie said. "She doesn't want us to know."

Mallie disagreed. How could they not speak of something so important? She tried to hold her tongue, but at dinner Sarah banged on her high chair, and Mallie began to cry. "We're sorry about the babies," she said.

Mother put her fork down. "Oh, my," she said. "I should have known you two were listening on the stairs."

"Why didn't you tell us?" Mallie asked. She wiped her nose with her napkin. "It's important."

Father cleared his throat.

"They overheard me talking to Mrs. Jenkins," Mother explained.

"It was not your business to listen," he said.

"But we did," Mallie said.

"We should have known," Hallie insisted.

Father rubbed his hand over his eyes. "The Lord giveth, and the Lord taketh away," he said.

"It's not fair!" Mallie cried.

Sarah began to wail. Mother patted her and gave her a piece of bread. "I'm sorry you listened to a private conversation," she said. "I would have told you in time, when I thought you were old enough to understand."

"We're old enough," Mallie said.

"You'll have to be," Mother said. "Your father is right. We must bend ourselves to the will of God."

Mallie thought that sounded harsh and cruel. But Mother continued, "I grew to think I might never have children. And then God sent me the two of you. Two babies at the same time. You were small, but you were perfect. And you lived. I couldn't have asked for a greater blessing or a greater happiness. You can't have good without bad, girls. You can't have loss without gain." She hugged Hallie, who sat beside her.

Mallie had never thought of herself as a baby

before. She pictured Mother lying in bed the way she had rested after Sarah was born, only with two babies, instead of one, cuddled beside her. She imagined herself and Hallie sharing a cradle. No greater happiness, Mother had said.

Comfort washed over Mallie. For the first time in months she felt at peace.

The next morning Mrs. Jenkins took them into her parlor. Two sheets of paper sat on the piano rack. They had notes drawn on them in pencil. "I wrote these out myself," Mrs. Jenkins said.

She played one. Mallie recognized it immediately—"Turkey in the Straw." Then Mrs. Jenkins played the other. Mallie's jaw dropped. The tune was very short and very simple—but it was, unmistakably, the "Moonlight" Sonata.

"It seemed important," Mrs. Jenkins said.

Mallie nodded. "It was."

On Sunday Mallie wore her navy sailor dress to church. Hallie and Sarah wore their white dresses. Hallie's now had navy trim.

"Nice dress, Mallie," Maude whispered as

they went in, "but I heard it was supposed to be red."

Mallie lifted her chin and stared Maude down. "You heard wrong," she said. "My mother made me this dress. It's exactly the way it's supposed to be."

27

Full Circle

Mallie knelt by the open window of her bedroom. A red leaf from the maple tree outside fell against her hands. She brushed it away. It was late August. The trees were changing color. The war was still going. School would start again soon.

One-two-three, one-two-three, Mallie counted in her head. She moved her fingers up and down on the smooth windowsill.

"Knitting circle time," Mother called up the stairs. Hallie jumped like a nervous cat.

Mallie rose slowly. "Don't fidget," she said.

"Easy for you to say," Hallie retorted.

"No, it isn't."

Hallie laughed. "Won't everyone be surprised?"

Downstairs they helped Mother load Sarah and the week's worth of knitting into the baby carriage. They started down the lane. The knitting circle was meeting at Mrs. Jenkins's house for the first time.

Mallie tried to walk slowly. "She's serving cherry pie," she said.

"I know," Mother replied. "Mrs. Jenkins said she was amazed at how hard you girls worked, helping her with the cherries. It was a nice way to make her feel welcome."

"We didn't mind." The cherries had stayed in season for weeks. Mallie had grown to hate the sight of them. Her hands were always reddish purple. Mother had to put bleach in the wash water to get them clean.

At Mrs. Jenkins's, Mallie tried to slip into the house unnoticed. "My goodness, here are the Graber twins," Mrs. Ellis sang out. Mallie wanted to scream. She was nervous enough without Mrs. Ellis carrying on.

Ruthie grinned. "My goodness," she said loudly, "they look exactly alike! What a surprise! And dressed alike, too!"

"Ruthie, hush," warned Mrs. Hawk. Mallie

stuck her tongue out at Ruthie. Ruthie laughed. Mallie felt better.

After they had heard the news of the chapter and knit bed socks for an hour, Mrs. Jenkins passed out the cherry pie. "Hallie and Mallie have offered to entertain us," she said.

Mallie saw Mother's head come up in surprise.

Hallie sat down at the piano and began to play. Mallie stood beside the bench. Her heart pounded. She tried to remember all the notes in her head. Mrs. Jenkins was a good and surprisingly patient teacher, but she had made them memorize their music. "You're both bright enough," she had said.

Hallie finished. The ladies applauded. Mallie didn't dare look at Mother. She slid into place, held her hands over the keyboard for a moment, and began to play. The quiet, beautiful music swirled around her. It seemed to end too soon. Mallie held the last note until the ladies began to clap again. Then she looked up.

Mother's smile filled the room.

28

Gypsy Red

"We wanted to please you," Hallie said on the walk home. She and Ruthie were full of laughter. Mallie was quiet.

"I am *very* pleased," Mother said. "I thought you didn't like the piano."

"I don't," Hallie said cheerfully. "But Mallie and I were sorry that we let you down. And Mrs. Jenkins was a good teacher."

Mallie said, "I want to keep playing. Forever."

Hallie stopped in her tracks. "But we don't want to," she said. "We finished what we planned to do."

Mother, Mrs. Hawk, and Ruthie all stopped, too. "*You* finished," Mallie said. "I didn't. I like the piano, and I want to keep playing."

Hallie didn't say anything.

"We're different," Mallie said. "You know we are. I've liked the piano all along."

Hallie grinned. Her chipped tooth showed. "I guess I knew you did," she said. "I guess any fool could tell."

"Mrs. Jenkins says she'll keep teaching me," Mallie said. "I already asked—if it's okay with you, Mother. She's a very good teacher. She has beginner music. We won't need to pay her. She says I can help her out plenty after—I mean, after—" Mallie stalled. Mrs. Jenkins had a secret of her own.

"After her baby comes," Mother finished for her. "I know about that. I suppose it would be a fair trade." She pushed Sarah's carriage forward. "Electa, can you keep Sarah for me tomorrow?"

"Of course," said Mrs. Hawk.

"The girls and I should go to Fort Wayne," said Mother. "They need new dresses for school, and we've only got two more weeks to make them up."

Mallie looked at Hallie. "Mother . . . ," they said together.

"Yes?"

"This time—" said Mallie.

"Please, if we help a lot with the sewing . . . ," said Hallie.

Mother looked at them. "You want to pick out the fabric yourselves."

"Yes, please," said Mallie.

Mother nodded. "You're old enough for that."

Hallie cleared her throat. "Do we have to match?"

Mother pushed the carriage faster. "No," she said almost carelessly. "I think we've moved beyond that, don't you?" She smiled.

Hallie swung Ruthie around in a circle, laughing. Mallie clapped her hands. She looked at the sycamore trees around her. Their leaves were orange and yellow against the blue sky. Mallie knew just what kind of dress she would have. It would be wool serge, with a dropped waist and plaited skirt. She would trim it with blue velveteen. And it would be bright, Gypsy red.

Author's Note

I based my earlier novel, *Ruthie's Gift,* on stories my grandmother Ruth Hawk Brubaker told me about her childhood. *Ruthie's Gift* was not a true story, but most of the things I included actually happened at one time or another to my grandmother and her six brothers.

One-of-a-Kind Mallie is different. Hallie and Mallie are fictional characters I created to be friends for Ruthie. I got to know them very well, and when I finished *Ruthie's Gift* I knew that Mallie, in particular, still had a lot to say. I wrote this book so that she could say it.

My grandmother remembers Gypsies camping on their farm every summer when she was a little girl. She told me a lot about the Gypsies. I found out more through the Indiana Folklore

Society. In 1970 a fieldworker collected and wrote down everything that people from one town could remember about Gypsies from their childhoods. The stories are remarkably consistent.

Gypsies still exist. They are shadowy people, and surprisingly little is known about them. Most of them originally came from Eastern Europe; many even now speak a language called Romany and have dark hair and eyes. But they came to America from many countries. They have different traditions and cannot all be lumped into one group.

Gypsy women have always told fortunes. In the early 1900s Gypsy men were often horse dealers, and sometimes they worked at pot mending or other odd jobs. They wandered across the country, first in horse-drawn wagons and later in cars. They stole from farms and businesses but were never involved in violent or large-scale crime. People considered them pests rather than true criminals.

Some of the other details in this story also came from my grandmother's memories. Mail-order brides such as Mrs. Jenkins were not as common in Indiana as they were in the West, where there weren't enough women for the men to marry. However, my grandmother remembers one farmer who did send away for a wife; she and her brothers called the woman "the Sears Roebuck bride."

Bass Farm, also known as Brookside, was a three-hundred-acre estate on the edge of Fort Wayne, the city nearest Cedarville. It belonged to Mr. John Bass, a wealthy investor. It had beautiful gardens, a deer and buffalo park, and a farm where prize horses and cattle were bred. My grandmother loved going on picnics there as a girl. The original house still stands; the land is now home to Saint Francis College.

Men from Cedarville would have gone to Fort Wayne to join the army. At the end of May 1917, two weeks after war was declared, the Fort Wayne district led the country in enlistments. A higher percentage of men from Allen County, Indiana, signed up to fight than from anywhere else in America. The local newspaper declared, "The nation turns to Fort Wayne today and salutes."

During the war, most men who didn't fight held jobs considered necessary to the war. Two of my great-uncles—both too young to join the army—made guns in a Philadelphia factory. Farming was necessary to the war because so much food was needed overseas; farmers were expected to grow more food with less manpower. Everyone grew vegetables in war gardens, and many schools had gardens of their own. In cities, vacant lots were turned into gardens for those who didn't own land.

Women often took the jobs left vacant by men. They worked in factories, shops, and offices. "If the call of war to men was 'to arms,' " says one publication from that time, "to women it was, 'to work!' " World War I marked the first time that large numbers of American women worked outside the home. Many other women volunteered for the war effort through organizations such as the Red Cross.

The American Red Cross was founded in 1882 as a disaster relief organization. It didn't gain national importance until 1916, when the country stood on the edge of war. Suddenly there was a great need for the services the Red Cross could provide. Local chapters sprang up everywhere. The Fort Wayne chapter was chartered on January 22, 1917, a few months before America entered the war. Membership dues were one dollar for adults, twenty-five cents for schoolchildren. Men and women joined in equal numbers, but women did more of the actual work. Being active in the Red Cross was a way that all women, even those with young children at home such as Mrs. Hawk and Mrs. Graber, could help with the war.

The Red Cross taught first aid, nursing, and hygiene and home care. Some women, such as Miss Lane in my story, worked during the day and taught Red Cross classes at night. Red Cross members staffed hospitals in America and abroad; Red Cross nurses went to war. Sewing and knitting circles made bandages and clothes in vast numbers and sent them overseas. In nine months the Fort Wayne Red Cross turned more than seventy-five thousand yards of flannel into bandages and sewed fifty thousand hospital gowns for injured soldiers. Knitting circle members ranged in age from six to ninety. The Red Cross raised money, too; its first fund drive in Allen County brought in $112,000 for war relief. At Christmas the Red Cross sent a small package—the size of a box of tissues—to every soldier at the front.

I know everything the Fort Wayne chapter of

the Red Cross did because of a woman named Isabelle H. Taylor. She understood something I believe strongly: that history happens as we live, and that the details of our everyday lives are as important to remember as the big battles fought to win wars. In 1919, at the end of what was called the "war to end all wars," Isabelle looked at the work she and others had done for the Red Cross and saw that it was good. She wrote a 150-page manuscript titled "War Work of the Fort Wayne Chapter of the American Red Cross." She typed it neatly, bound it in leather, and gave it to the library. Eighty years later it was there for me to read. The last line of her introduction reads, "It is the truth, and if not impeccably told, it still is history."